Kimberly dabbed a nervous tongue to her lip

The gesture grabbed Nigel's attention, sharpened the pull between them. Following the bad-boy rules she had set out earlier, he moved slowly across the bar toward her, stopping directly in front of her chair.

She looked up, her lips parted as though to speak. Instead, she fluttered her fingers to the top button on her blouse.

He shifted closer, his knee brushing hers. The accidental touch triggered small fires over his skin. And from the flush on her cheeks, he could see she felt it, too. The unspoken desire in her eyes made him bold. He slid one arm around her waist and pulled her to him, feeling her swollen breasts against his body. She shivered.

In his best bad-boy tone he leaned forward and whispered hotly into her ear, "I want you."

ROMANCE

Dear Reader,

Many of you have asked about the hunky, former professional wrestler Nigel—aka "The Phantom" with the body of The Rock and the heart of E.T.—who loved to bake brownies for the heroine in *Joyride* (Harlequin Temptation #867, February 2002).

Well, Nigel's back and he's bad.

Make that *almost* bad. In *Building a Bad Boy,* Nigel has decided he'll never win the woman of his dreams by sitting next to the phone, so he signs up with a dating agency whose owner, Kimberly Logan, enrolls him in her "How To Make a Bad Boy" program. After all, women love bad boys, right?

What Kimberly is totally unprepared for is the impact her coaching has...on her!

This is one of my last books for Harlequin Temptation, and I'll miss the line as both a reader and writer. My history with this series goes back to 1992 when, as an unpublished author, my story placed second in their fifth annual Harlequin Temptation contest. I finally sold to Harlequin four years later.

I hope you enjoy *Building a Bad Boy.* To check out my upcoming books and enter my monthly contests, please visit my Web site, www.colleencollins.net.

Happy reading!

Colleen Collins

Books by Colleen Collins

HARLEQUIN TEMPTATION
867—JOYRIDE
899—TONGUE-TIED
913—LIGHTNING STRIKES
939—TOO CLOSE FOR COMFORT
977—SWEET TALKIN' GUY*

*The Spirits Are Willing

HARLEQUIN DUETS
10—MARRIED AFTER
    BREAKFAST
22—ROUGH AND RUGGED
30—IN BED WITH THE PIRATE
39—SHE'S GOT MAIL!
108—LET IT BREE
    CAN'T BUY ME LOUIE

COLLEEN COLLINS
Building A Bad Boy

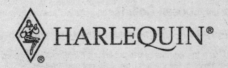

HARLEQUIN®

TORONTO • NEW YORK • LONDON
AMSTERDAM • PARIS • SYDNEY • HAMBURG
STOCKHOLM • ATHENS • TOKYO • MILAN • MADRID
PRAGUE • WARSAW • BUDAPEST • AUCKLAND

To the Temptresses

ISBN 0-373-69216-1

BUILDING A BAD BOY

This edition published by arrangement with Harlequin Books S.A.

® and TM are trademarks of the publisher. Trademarks indicated with ® are registered in the United States Patent and Trademark Office, the Canadian Trade Marks Office and in other countries.

www.eHarlequin.com

Printed in U.S.A.

1

KIMBERLY LOGAN PUSHED OPEN the polished mahogany door with the stenciled words *Life Dates...* where you're coached along the path to love. The buzz of Las Vegas traffic faded as she stepped inside and clicked the door shut behind her. She paused to catch her breath while eyeing the recent renovation of her waiting room from cheery yellow to seductive dusty rose. The new color scheme was infinitely more stimulating, exciting...precisely the environment Kimberly wanted for her clientele who came seeking love ever after and lust evermore.

The air-conditioning seemed a tad cool, though. Even in February, she liked to keep it humming on a low setting. Most dating service first-timers were anxious. Cool air helped soothe them. Too chilly, however, would only add to their nervousness.

I'll ask Maurice to adjust the temperature ASAP. Kimberly headed to his desk—her high heels clicking across the polished parquet floor until she stepped onto the thick Oriental rug—and halted at a teak desk.

Behind which sat Maurice, his tanned face creased

by his I'm-not-happy-with-you look. Despite his attitude, he looked natty as usual. Khaki pants, pink polo shirt. Gay men sure knew how to dress.

She glanced at her office door, which was closed. "I know," she demurred, meeting her office manager's gaze. "I'm late."

"Kimberly," he said crisply, "you *must* stop making appointments for 9:00 a.m. and not showing up until—" with a flourish of his wrist, he checked the time "—9:38. Worse, this guy showed up fifteen minutes early, so he's been cooling his heels in your office for almost an hour. Fortunately he has the patience of a saint, unlike that guy two weeks ago who copped a 'tude and used your Waterford bowl for an ashtray—"

"It's those weekly Chamber of Commerce breakfast meetings," she said on a release of breath. "People arrive late, speakers talk too long. I'm on time for all my other meetings."

"When you're *here*, not cavorting about in your Beemer, doing *networking* things."

"You're right. I'm still reacting to Great Dates opening up one of their national offices two blocks away. I keep thinking if I don't do everything to promote Life Dates, especially as it has such a similar name, they'll cut into our business."

"Kimberly, what you offer is unique. No global dating agency can begin to cater to Vegas clients the way you do. They're like Hershey's chocolate, you're like Francine's Gourmet Bonbons."

Francine, a local high-end chocolatier, had a loyal following who thought nothing of shelling out twenty-four dollars for a dozen homemade, hand-dipped bonbons.

"Thanks," Kimberly murmured.

It offered some comfort that Life Dates was the most successful dating agency in Vegas, although she had a lot on her plate running the business as well as being its resident "success coach"—a marketing term she'd coined four years ago when she opened the doors. As a success coach, she didn't just play the same boring connect-the-dots and match up person A with B, like Great Dates did, she personally *coached* her clients—from picking out their clothes to helping them practice the fine art of dating and, ultimately, seduction.

"If it makes you feel any better," said Maurice, "I set up a meeting next week with Barnet and Owens."

"The advertising agency?"

"Yes. They're going to pitch a local TV campaign idea for us."

"Great idea." She plucked a jelly bean from the jar on his desk.

"You didn't eat at the breakfast meeting, did you?"

"No time."

He handed her a clipboard with a form secured underneath a silver clamp. "Here's his application."

She quickly scanned it. "His first name's *Nigel*."

"*So* Noel Coward, isn't it? You know, I should fill that candy bowl with soy nuts instead of sugar. No wonder you're always motoring a thousand miles an hour."

"Nigel *Durand*."

"A little English, a little French." Maurice lowered his voice. "Shame he's straight."

She peeked at Maurice over the clipboard.

He raised a hand in mock protest. "I'd never flirt with any of your clientele." He feigned a shudder. "I might be gay, but I'm no masochist."

Kimberly offered a small smile.

"It's good to see you smile," he said warmly. "Someday I'll even get you to laugh out loud."

She returned to the application. "*Wrestler?*"

"Former. Plus he's bald, thirty-four, wants the picket fence, wife, kids."

She looked up and frowned. "Bald?"

"Retro-Yul Brynner. *Very* in right now."

"Hairless heads are making a comeback?" she murmured, nudging a strand of her blond hair back into her chignon.

"Darling, you might *run* the chicest dating service this side of the Rockies, but you *must* get out more! Go see a Vin Diesel flick."

Vin who? "No time." She checked her reflection in the gold-veined mirror over the guest couch. Making a quick adjustment to her jacket, she murmured, "I'll go in and meet Nigel now."

"I'll bring in your coffee."

"Two—"

"I know. Black. Two packets Skinny Sweet."

She headed to her office. "And by the way," she whispered over her shoulder. "I laugh out loud sometimes."

"When?"

"*I Love Lucy* reruns."

Maurice tossed her a "really?" look as he sauntered back to the kitchenette.

Until he came along, she'd been through nearly a dozen office assistants. It wasn't that Kimberly was overly demanding or intense—despite what several of them had huffed—she just wanted her business to be run *right*.

Which, finally, Maurice did. After almost a year working together, she didn't know what she'd do without him. Even his nagging. The guy had her best interests at heart.

Unlike the other men she'd had in her life.

She placed her hand on the brass knob of her office door, took a calming breath, then opened it and stepped inside.

"Mr. Durand, I'm so very sorry." Kimberly swept into the room as she had a hundred times before, shoulders back, chin high, exuding conviction. She'd learned long ago that no matter what the circumstances, people responded favorably to grand displays of confidence.

"I had an emergency meeting this morning that was impossible to break," she continued, putting on her best I'm-so-sorry look. "I apologize for your having to wait."

Nigel Durand rose from the guest chair. And kept rising until he'd unfolded into a towering mass of bulk that loomed over her.

A towering mass of bulk with a shiny dome on top.

She eased in a stream of air and stared heavenward, getting the giddy sense she was standing at the foot of a mountain. And for a moment, she felt small, overwhelmed. Things Kimberly Logan *never* felt.

"That's all right, ma'am," said a deep voice that reverberated like thunder from the mountaintop.

She felt like telling him she was only twenty-eight. Call her Miss or Ms., but please not ma'am.

She blinked at the mountaintop, recalling Maurice's reference to a retro-Yul Brynner. A distant memory of the movie *The King and I* flitted through her mind. As the king of Siam, Yul had swaggered across his palace, oozing arrogance and testosterone out of every pore.

Maurice was right. Bald heads *were* sexy. She wondered how it would feel to run her fingers over Nigel's smooth dome....

An unexpected shiver of anticipation ran down her spine.

"Please, Mr. Durand," she said, surprised how breathy her voice suddenly sounded, "have a seat."

As the mountain descended, she crossed behind her chrome-and-glass desk. "Let's talk about how Life Dates can help you find the woman of your dreams." She sat down in her high-back, ergonomic chair, and set the clipboard on the desk. She hoped

Maurice showed up soon with the coffee—her energy was flagging.

Nigel settled back into the guest chair facing her, and she locked on his eyes. *Such a rich blue.* Like the irises that grew rampant in her neighbor's field back in Sterling, Colorado. As a child, she loved to pick armfuls and arrange them in her favorite vase. The vibrant colors brightened a home dominated by her serious, hardworking father.

"So Mr. Durand," Kimberly said, folding her hands neatly in front of her. "You were a professional wrestler?"

"Yes."

She nodded, waiting for him to say more. Nothing. Finally, she broke the silence. "Where did you practice this profession?"

"A fledgling career as a college football star segued into wrestling. Started out touring the circuits, got invited into the Showcase of the Immortals. Eventually made the grade into the WWE, settled in Vegas."

"WWE stands for…"

"World Wrestling Entertainment. Retired from the ring a year ago." He shifted in his seat, which would be a small movement on anyone else. But on Nigel, muscles bulged and strained before the mass stilled.

She took a calming breath, which had an absolutely zero calming effect. "How about I put on some music," she suddenly said, her voice doing that breathy thing again. Good thing she forgot to ask

Maurice to turn down the air-conditioning. Right now her overheated body needed every blast of chill she could get.

"Yes, music," she answered herself a bit too enthusiastically. "Let's put some on."

She got up and went to the CD player that sat on a carved walnut bookcase in the corner. Music helped people relax. It better help her relax, anyway. She began flipping through the discs. "Tony Bennett? Lyle Lovett? Disco Divas?" *Disco Divas?* Had to be a recent Maurice addition.

"Got any Celine Dion?"

She glanced over her shoulder at Nigel. "You're kidding—" She stopped, seeing the serious expression on his face. "Uh, let me look… I'm sure we have something here…." She'd just broken one of her cardinal rules about never insulting a client. Today was not starting out well.

"Here's one!" she finally announced. "*The Colour of My Love,*" she read off the front of the CD.

"Yeah, that one's cool."

Not too many men admitted to being Celine Dion fans. It was like admitting they cried at sad movies. Or loved to go shopping.

After sliding the disc into the player, Kimberly headed back to her desk. Celine's clear, vibrant voice filled the room, singing about always being there for her man.

Kimberly sat down, remembering a time she believed that. She still believed in true love for *others,* just not for herself. It was a good philosophy, though, because not being romantically enmeshed kept her focused on her priorities. Number one being her independence—financial, personal, professional. Number two being... Well, she hadn't gotten that far yet.

She glanced at the door. Where *was* Maurice and her coffee?

She grabbed a pencil out of her ceramic cup and fiddled with it, feeling jittery, wishing Nigel wouldn't stare at her like that. Those big blue eyes had a way of boring into her, as though they saw more than she was willing to let on. Probably a technique he used in his wrestling days, a psychological tactic to unnerve his opponent.

"So," she said, determined to *not* be unnerved. *I should ask him something about wrestling.* Like what? All she knew about wrestling was big, muscled bodies and bone-crunching antics.

Her gaze dropped to Nigel's T-shirt decorated with the faded image of a...

"Rooster?" she blurted.

The corners of his eyes crinkled when he smiled. "Foghorn Leghorn."

"Foghorn...? Was that...your wrestling name?"

He did a double take, then laughed. His lips were so full, his teeth so big.

"Didn't you watch cartoons when you were a kid?" he asked.

"No."

"Not even on Saturday mornings?"

Saturday mornings were like any other morning in her house. They had to be quiet because her mother was sick. Rather than watch TV, Kimberly would sit on the porch and read. Or hang out at her neighbor's, helping feed or groom the horses.

"No," she answered softly.

"Really? I thought all kids knew Foghorn Leghorn. He's a cartoon character. My kid sisters decided, years ago, that I was like him because I'm so big and my voice is so deep."

Yes, you are big. Mountain-size big. A woman probably got lost in those arms, cocooned within all those muscles and warmth. "So," she whispered, "what was your professional name?"

"The Phantom."

She sucked in a breath of surprise. "The Phantom who pitched trucks a few years back?"

When he nodded yes her heartbeat pounded so hard, she feared it would overpower Celine. Kimberly clutched the pencil, recalling the series of television commercials starring The Phantom. She'd seen them late at night while catching up on paperwork. She'd never been all that hooked on TV, but whenever The Phantom had appeared, she'd been riveted. He exuded strength and mystery…and was one hell of a piece of eye candy.

No wonder she didn't recognize him. In those ads, he wore a black mask à la Zorro. His only other body covering had been a pair of leather briefs that covered the essentials but left the rest of his massive, muscled body deliciously exposed. He'd been a mouthwatering mound of chiseled, oiled brown…

Crack.

She looked down at the pencil she'd just snapped in two.

"You okay?" Nigel asked.

Kimberly raised her gaze and met those eyes, wide with concern. Heat rushed to her cheeks as she nonchalantly dropped the broken pencil pieces into the chrome trash can beneath her desk where they clattered loudly in their descent. Maurice was too efficient, checking her wastebasket—among other things—every morning when he got in, taking care of anything the night cleaning crew had lazily forgotten. Really, Maurice was too on top of things. She'd have a talk with him about leaving a little trash, just enough to deaden the sounds of things tossed in moments of embarrassment.

Like snapped-in-two pencils.

"What were those trucks called?" she asked as though nothing out of the usual had just happened.

He frowned again. "What trucks?"

"The ones in The Phantom ad."

"The Crusher."

Oh *yessss,* now she remembered. In one of the ads, he'd wrapped his arms around a truck—crushed it to his massive, bulky chest—and it had morphed into a sleek, sexy woman moaning his name. He'd then carried the damsel across the city, through burning buildings, over long hot stretches of sizzling desert. And the voice-over had said, "The Crusher. In its embrace, you'll remain safe, protected."

Thousands of women had purchased those trucks.

When those commercials were running, Kimberly had lost count of the number of her female clients who'd said they'd *love* to meet a man like The Phantom. A man who was outrageously bad while defiantly good.

"Where's The Phantom these days?" Kimberly's eyes dipped to that rooster, wondering what Nigel's chest looked like underneath. Did he still shave? Was he one big mass of brown, oiled muscle?

"He doesn't exist except in people's fantasies."

"What a shame," she murmured. "Women love that kind of man."

"Women love James Bond, too," he snapped, "but that doesn't mean he exists."

She shifted in her seat. Kimberly had obviously stumbled into some serious button-pushing territory. "I'm not talking about everyday *reality*," she said, keeping her voice conversational. "I'm talking about *mystery*."

"Mystery?" He cocked an eyebrow. "You mean, *faking* something you're not."

"No," she said slowly, "I'm talking about adopting a persona that appeals to the opposite sex. Dating is a buyer's market and women want to 'buy' a man who exudes a virile, forbidden, bad-boy persona."

He frowned. "Maybe they love the persona, but they don't want the man behind it."

"That's ridiculous."

"*That's* the true reality, Ms. Logan. I should know. I lived it."

Kimberly realized she was tense, leaning forward in her own chair. Nigel was sitting stiffly, his big square knuckles gripping the arms of his chair. Their gazes were locked, waiting for one of them to back down.

The door opened and Maurice entered, carrying a steaming pink flamingo coffee cup. "Sorry this took so long," he said, sashaying across the room to Kimberly's desk.

"Was wondering where you were," she said, hearing the edge to her voice. But this little surprise showdown with Nigel had left her tense.

"Couldn't find the Skinny Sweet. Had to do a quick trip next door to the convenience store. Figured while I was there, might as well grab something nutritional for your breakfast, too." He set down a steaming foil-wrapped package that reeked of onions and spice.

She shot him a questioning look.

"Tofu breakfast burrito." He twirled a finger in a circle. "Wrapped in a whole-wheat tortilla."

Her mouth dropped open slightly. "You're kidding."

"No, and you're welcome." Maurice folded his hands neatly. "Anything else before I go?"

Kimberly caught herself and smiled tightly at Nigel. "Did you care for anything?"

"No, thanks."

With a pleasant dip of his head at Kimberly, Maurice left.

Nigel fought the urge to follow the assistant out of the office. This interview was growing increasingly frustrating, just like all his dating experiences. And bringing up The Crusher commercial pissed him off. If there was anything he regretted doing in his life, it was that. As a wrestler, he'd been flexing his skills at least. In that commercial, he'd been nothing but a piece of oiled meat.

Celine wailed about her man reaching for her, and being all that she could for him....

Nigel eased out a slow breath. *That's* all he wanted, too. A woman who would reach for him, love him for who he was. And he'd give her the same...and more. His heart, his love for the rest of their days. *If I walk out now, I might lose that chance.* Up to now, he'd tried everything—slipping women his number, writing a personal ad, baking brownies as gifts—and every time, he failed at love. Walking in the Life Dates door was his last chance for love.

Can't leave. Can't give up, not yet. Ms. Right was somewhere out there, he just needed help finding her.

Although to look at Kimberly Logan, it was difficult to imagine this woman being a matchmaker. From the moment she'd sailed through the door, she'd seemed more like a machine than flesh and blood. Most women wearing a silk suit looked soft, feminine. Even though it was a nice shade of purple, it fit her like a suit of armor. That bun number only added to her strict look.

Snapping that pencil in two cinched it, though. This was a woman who needed some serious loosening up.

A woman who, also, from that perplexed look on her face, might appreciate an explanation for his strong reaction to that damn commercial. It'd be in his favor, too. If she understood what turned his crank, she'd know what to leave alone.

"I hated that commercial," he muttered.

She arched an eyebrow.

He scrubbed a hand across his face. "That image— me looking like a meatball Zorro with a woman in my arms—is the last image the public has of The Phantom. Feels rotten for that to be my parting shot, you know? It's my biggest regret in life, something I'll never repeat again."

She nodded, all poise and sophistication.

Reminded him of women from his past. The coiffed, moneyed ones who hung out ringside during matches and tipped their way backstage afterward. Women who were privileged, uptight and desperate for some guy they viewed as wild and bad to help them relax a little. He'd made the mistake of indulging a few of them, then realized their game. They didn't want him.

They wanted The Phantom.

"So," said Kimberly, pushing the burrito aside with her manicured pink nails. "Who is that man they discovered?"

"Pardon?"

"You said that women might love the persona, but not desire the man behind it," she prompted. "And I was wondering, who did they discover behind the mask? I need to know you, understand your dating history so we can plan our strategy. That's how we differ from other agencies, and why our success rate is so high. I'm your success coach, as you probably read in our ad. In that capacity, I work closely with you, get to know you, so I can maximize our approach for *your* success."

Her clipped, assured tone was as smooth and polished as the furniture in this room. The only soft thing in the area was the sunlight from a corner window sifting through a ficus tree, creating a pattern of light and leaves on the floor as delicate as lace.

Plus, there was nothing personal in here. No family pictures, kids' finger paintings, *nothing* to show she had a life other than work.

"Women didn't like the homebody," he admitted.

She raised her eyebrows, a signal for him to elaborate.

"Homebody," he muttered, shifting in his seat. "You know, the guy who bakes brownies. Wants the picket fence and two-point-five kids."

"I can't imagine any woman not wanting that…"

"Oh, I can." He snorted a laugh. "Nice guys finish last."

"May I suggest," she said gently, "that you're a nice guy who maybe tries too hard?"

That hurt almost as much as a ringside body slam. "Baking brownies is trying too hard?"

"What do you do at night...besides bake?"

"Sit in my favorite armchair, listen to music. Watch cable if a good movie's on."

"While waiting by the phone."

He shifted in his seat. "No."

"Where's the phone?"

"Next to the armchair." Okay, she was smart. Uptight, but smart.

"You're too available," she said quietly. "People don't respect someone who's at their beck and call." Her eyes softened, their pewter color shifting to a soft gray, and he wondered if she had firsthand experience in this area.

She took a sip of her coffee and set it down. "We need to make you more...unattainable."

Kimberly jotted a note on the application, then put down her pen. "I have an approach that would work excellently for you. I've used it before with men and they've all ended up married to the woman of their fantasies within a year. I call it my Bad Boy Makeover."

He frowned. He knew it. These regimented types always loved the bad boys. "I don't want to be bad."

"Wasn't The Phantom bad?"

"He was known for defeating evil, saving the woman."

"We'll be doing something similar. Women eat it up. You'll have to turn the ringer off on your phone because so many of them will be calling you." She opened a drawer. "Let me get my notes, explain in a bit more detail."

She extracted a navy-blue folder. "Here we go!" she said, opening it. "Step one," she read. "Look like a bad boy. Step two, act like a bad boy. Step three, make women melt. Step four, kiss her 'til she whimpers. Step five, love her 'til she screams. Step six, pick 'the One.'"

He blinked, digesting the stream of words, all punctuated with bad-boy this and that. He'd once dated a woman who loved writing "Honey-Do" lists, which had struck him as odd considering all she needed to do was ask him for help and he'd be there.

But this success coach's bad-boy list was stupid. A perversion of a honey-do list. If you want a honey, do this. And this. What was step five? Love her 'til she screams? This edgy, armored broad thought *she* was going to teach *him* how to do that?

Was she freaking crazy?

He tapped his finger on the chair of the arm, figuring he could be out of her office and back on the street in ten strides.

Last chance for love, buddy.

He cleared his throat, rubbed a spot on his forehead. "And, uh, these work?"

"I've had an eighty-five percent success rate. Like I said, women love bad boys." She leaned forward, a seductive look softening her features.

And for a moment, he saw something he liked in

her. Something tender, almost needy. The opposite of everything she plastered on her earnest, coiffed self. And in that moment, he had a flash of understanding about this woman. Just as she externally made over others, she'd done so with herself.

And he wondered what was so soft, so vulnerable inside that she'd built this fortress of a person.

"I can make you over in three months," she said.

Three months? In ninety days, he finally might have the one thing that had eluded him all these years. A loving partner, someone with whom to share his life, his dreams. A woman he could coddle and pamper and love for the rest of his life.

But a makeover?

Celine wailed about never finding love again.

"I'll do it," said Nigel.

2

Step one: Look like a bad boy

"Look like a bad boy," Nigel muttered to himself the next morning, giving his head a slow shake. He thought back to all the times he'd made one of his three kid sisters go back to her room and change clothes that were too tight, too low cut, too short before leaving the house. How many times had he reprimanded them, "Dressing bad isn't good." Who knew those words would come back to haunt him.

Come to find out, once you were grown-up, dressing bad *was* good.

But he still wouldn't change a thing about how he treated his kid sisters, despite their eye rolling and occasional pouts. With their father working swing shift at the factory, their big brother, Nigel, had often had to play "Dad."

Even their boyfriends did as he told.

And not just because Nigel was merely the big brother.

He was just plain big.

By twenty, he was six-five, two-hundred-and-eighty pounds of rock-hard muscle thanks to his daily workouts and amateur wrestling schedule. The brave young men who dated his sisters were more than willing to let Nigel be the law of the land. If he said to have his sister home by midnight, the kid pulled up in the driveway at 11:50.

Speaking of time, Nigel glanced at the wall clock again. This shop for tall men, aptly named Tall Threads, had a clock on the wall shaped like a pair of extra-long pants, with suspenders for hands. The shorter suspender pointed at nine, the longer at three.

Nine-fifteen.

Maybe he could scare teenage kids into being on time, but apparently it didn't work with Ms. Kimberly Logan.

Yesterday, he'd thought she was joking when, while escorting him out after his interview, she'd announced she'd meet him at Tall Threads at 9:00 a.m. the following morning. She explained it'd be their first "success coach" meeting where they'd shop for bad-boy clothes.

He'd laughed.

She hadn't.

With a pinched "this is serious" look, she reminded him that twenty percent of his fee, as outlined in the contract he'd signed, was allocated for miscellaneous expenditures.

Which, in this case, meant clothes to build his bad-boy image.

He had the urge to ask if she shopped someplace special to build her uptight-woman image, but had bitten his tongue. Not only because his mother had drilled it into him to never insult a lady, but also because once he'd made a commitment, he stuck to it. His siblings had the same trait; the roots from witnessing their parents' living commitment to their faith, their marriage, their children. They'd soon be celebrating their fortieth wedding anniversary, a milestone Nigel wished for himself, someday.

"Look like a bad boy," he muttered to himself for the nth time. If his mother knew he'd gone to these lengths, she'd cross herself and say at least a dozen Hail Marys.

Through the store display window, he suddenly saw Kimberly striding purposefully down the sidewalk, dressed in a classy but strict-looking pantsuit. Bright red, which surprised him. She seemed the kind of woman to stick with cooler colors to match that attitude of hers.

Sunlight glinted off her hair, making the blond appear almost white. As she walked, she talked on a cell phone, the fingers of her free hand gesturing emphatically.

The woman was a whirlwind. He wondered if she ever relaxed…or even knew how to.

She glanced at her wristwatch, visibly jumped and quickly ended the call. Then she checked her reflection in the window, tucking a stray hair into another variation of that bun-thing she called a hairdo. After a quick adjustment to her jacket, she plastered on a smile and sailed into the store.

He shook his head. *The lady has perfected her grand entrance.* Having been a professional wrestler, grand entrances were something he knew a thing or two about and she certainly had hers down.

Blinking rapidly, she approached a salesclerk and began talking animatedly.

Taking in a fortifying breath, Nigel sauntered up to her. She did a double take, then replastered on that manufactured smile.

"Nigel! I apologize for being late. I had a morning meeting—"

"Let's get this over with." He'd already heard her "I had a morning meeting" speech yesterday. Just because he'd made a commitment to this shopping gig didn't mean he had to be good-natured about it.

"Bad mood?"

"Goes with the bad boy."

She looked surprised.

"It was a joke."

"Oh. Right." Scarcely missing a beat, she resumed issuing instructions to the clerk, a middle-aged guy with thinning hair and a cat-that-ate-the-canary grin.

"And some of those stretchy T-shirts," Kimberly said, her voice rushing over words, "any color but pink. And you have leather jackets, right?"

"I'm not wearing a leather jacket," Nigel interjected.

The clerk cocked an eyebrow at Kimberly as though to say "Do I listen to him or you?"

She gave him an authoritative nod. He sauntered away.

Kimberly leaned toward Nigel. "I'm only asking you to try a few on," she said under her breath. "Besides, if you check out the price tags, this place is *very* reasonable."

"That's not the issue." Nigel had handled his pro-wrestling earnings well. Tack on his subsequent earnings from endorsements and coaching, he never worried about money. He opened his mouth to say more about not wanting to drape himself in leather when her perfume snagged his attention.

He recalled the spicy scent from yesterday. But today, he picked up a trace of something extra. Something hot and languid, like a drop of summer.

The scent seemed too exotic compared to the rest of her strict look, which made Nigel wonder if she was like one of those hothouse orchids. Elegantly beautiful, but needing a humid environment in which to thrive.

"Vegas isn't a leather-jacket kinda town," he said, finally gathering his thoughts. "Men wear sport shirts, linen jackets."

"Leather equates to sex. Besides, it's only February. Still cool enough to wear one."

Sex. Not that he hadn't heard the word before. Or didn't give it as much, if not more, respect than he did money. But to hear this exotic orchid *say* the word so matter-of-factly was like hearing Queen Elizabeth cuss.

"I thought…" he backpedaled, grappling to remember what he'd been thinking before "sex" entered the picture "…this was about getting a date, not getting…" *laid.* Maybe she could casually say "sex" as though it were a refreshing after-dinner mint, but he didn't talk that way. Maybe it was a dying art, but a man watched his language and his behavior around ladies.

"Hopefully one leads to the other," she added, filling in the missing blank.

"I like to wait for the…*other.*"

"Well, that's certainly your prerogative," she answered, raising one shapely eyebrow. "But my business is to sell you, and trust me, sex sells. And by that I mean, we're working on you *oozing* sex, flashing enough testosterone to bring women to their knees. Figuratively speaking, of course."

He stared at those red lips that uttered things like "sex" and "knees." They were still moving but he'd stopped listening. Had he ever before seen such a perfectly shaped mouth? Outlined and glossed as though it was an art object and not a living, pulsing piece of her body. Funny, she talked so straightforwardly about bad boys and sex and "figurative" whatevers, but he didn't detect the source of her own passion.

Had to be hidden deep somewhere under that fire-engine red suit.

"So what do you think?" she said.

He lifted his gaze to meet her gray eyes. "I've never worn a leather jacket before," he murmured, fairly certain that the response would fit just about anything she'd been saying.

"You wore a leather Speedo."

Not this again. "As *The Phantom*. Not me."

"Like he's not part of you."

"Like he was a *character*, somebody I made up." His voice hardened. "I'm getting tired of resurrecting The Phantom every time we meet." If she brought up that commercial again, he'd walk.

Their gazes locked for a long moment. Over the speakers a singer crooned the old Dylan tune "Tangled Up In Blue," wailing about a man keepin' on, like a bird that flew, tangled up in blue.

That's me, thought Nigel. Tangled up in this, committed to this. My best bet is not to fight it, but flow with it if I want to find true love.

She seemed to pick up on his thoughts because her face relaxed a bit, her mouth mimicking a smile.

"We haven't even said hello and we're already off on the wrong foot," she said, her voice taking on a syrupy quality. She extended her hand. "Hello."

He hadn't noticed her watch yesterday. Ornate. Silver. Were those diamonds? Either she had a money-eyed beau or she bought this bauble for herself. He voted for the latter. Only women who made big bucks could afford such luxuries, which meant she'd successfully played matchmaker to many "life dates."

Which meant those people were, at this moment, happily attached—maybe even married—to their soul mates.

Which meant it was in his best interests to stick with the program. Even if he felt tangled up in blue.

He took her hand, which disappeared into his. "Hello."

"We're getting silly over a jacket."

When she turned her head slightly, he noticed she wore only one earring. Fancy watch, but only one earring. There was no beau in her life. Not a live-in one, anyway. Because a loving man would stop her before she rushed out the door missing an earring, or anything else for that matter.

And a really good man would grab this bundle of energy on her way out the door and plant a kiss on those luscious red lips so they didn't look *too* perfect.

"The leather jacket is about first impressions, that's all," the glossy red lips continued. "And first impressions are *the* most important thing in the dating scene. Actually, the most important thing in any scene. Anyway, the dating scene is a buyer's market and we're making you into a salable product. Once you're off the shelf, you'll have plenty of time to let the woman of your dreams—your *life date*—get to know the real you, see into your heart, and fall in love with you and only you—"

Her voice caught, and he sensed she'd just revealed more than she'd intended. Someone hadn't loved her, *only* her?

"You know what?" she asked, rushing on, "I think you'll need a new, *bad* name to go along with the your new, bad look."

He frowned. "I thought this meeting was about my *looking* like a bad boy, not taking the name of one."

"Yes, but wouldn't it have been silly to have named the Eiffel Tower 'that big pointy structure'?"

He paused. "I'm not a building."

Her gaze traveled down his body, then back up. When she met his eyes, he noticed a pink tinge to her cheeks.

"No, no you're not a building," she finally said. Her fingers fluttered around the top button of her silk blouse.

"What's wrong with Nigel?"

She continued playing with the button. "Nigel is so...Noel Coward."

"Noel who?"

"It's too stuffy." She closed her eyes and rolled the button between her thumb and forefinger. "Got it!" she suddenly said, releasing the button to snap her fingers. "Your name will be...Nicky!"

"*Nicky?*"

"Yes," she enthused. "Nicky Durand!" She shuddered a breath. "It's sexy, bad...oh, yes, very bad, which is very good. Nicky it is."

Before hearing that burst of breathy enthusiasm, he'd been ready to fight to the death to remain Nigel...but suddenly "Nicky" wasn't so bad. Especially if women reacted as she did, all pink cheeked and ready to pop buttons.

"I'll just say it's my nickname, right?" Lots of people had nicknames.

"Hmm, yes." She looked around, distracted.

"After a few meet and greets with a woman, I'll divulge my true name."

"Right, right," she murmured, catching the eye of the salesclerk, who was thumbing through a rack of leather jackets. "Black," she called out. "Lots of zippers."

She reached into her jacket pocket and extracted a yellow jelly bean, which she tossed into her mouth.

Yeah, she lived alone. Nobody to watch over her, make sure she ate right. Nigel could see it now—her running out the door in the mornings missing earrings, stuffing her pockets with pieces of candy. He doubted she had a pet or plants—when would there be time to take care of them?

Which meant there was no one to come home to, to talk to about her day, share her worries and her joys. Did women like her really choose such lifestyles, or did they wake up one day and realize they'd worked so hard to make their way in the world, they'd forgotten to make a home for themselves?

The thought saddened him. Because he related. His home life had been loving, but money had been tight so his dad was always pulling double shifts. And even though Nigel knew firsthand how much he, his sisters and Mom missed him—or how many school events he missed—damn if Nigel didn't do the same thing.

By the age of twenty-four, he had been on the road building his wrestling career, figuring there was plenty of time for marriage and babies. Then he got sidelined with that busted knee, which gave him plenty of time to realize he'd let his career deep-six building his own family. The fact hit him hardest after being released from the hospital and there was no loving woman welcoming him home, no child's arms hugging him, just his empty apartment.

"How are these, ma'am?" The salesclerk walked up, his arms laden with jeans and shirts. "Left several leather jackets in the dressing room." He slid a glance to Nigel. "Lightweight ones."

Kimberly went into success-coach mode and began flipping through the clothes, oohing over this, saying "no" to that. Nigel stood nearby until the salesclerk escorted him to a dressing room.

It was a big room. No surprise there, considering this place catered to big guys. Alone, Nigel looked at himself in the mirror. Today he'd thrown on a pair of old cotton shorts, a loose T that had been washed so many times he wasn't sure if the logo was from a burger joint he once visited in Minnesota or another Foghorn Leghorn that had seen better days. On his feet, an old pair of sandals that had turned the color of dirt.

Hardly chick-magnet attire.

Maybe he'd come in here muttering to himself about "looking like a bad boy," but faced with his image, he had to admit this let's-go-bowling look needed some serious renovation. How many times had he seen his buddies dress like wolves when they were on the prowl? Tight pants, body-hugging shirts, slick shoes. Even his best pal Rigo, now settled down with a bambino on the way, had donned that look in his bachelor days.

Looking hot and bad to attract the opposite sex.

"Maybe you bake the best brownies in the state of Nevada," he said to his reflection, "but buddy, you sure aren't cooking up everlasting love." He started peeling off his clothes, ready to dress bad.

He'd just kicked aside his shorts when a woman's voice called out, "How's it going?"

He straightened and saw Kimberly's face peeking through the curtain of his dressing room.

"What the hell are you doing?" He released a huff of breath. "Sorry."

"For what?"

"Cussing."

She blinked. "Everybody cusses sometime."

"I try not to. Made a point to watch my language when helping raise my three kid sisters. Role model and all that." He pressed his thumb against his lower lip. "What are you doing here?"

"I wanted to check up on you."

"I'm naked."

Her eyes dipped. "Not quite. You're wearing…"

Kimberly couldn't stop staring at the bulging black briefs that seemed stretched to the max over his member. Just like that black leather Speedo number he wore in those Crusher ads. She glanced at his oversize feet. So what they said was true….

She tried to look back at his face, but there was a lot of body to cover on the way. Prominent thigh muscles. Ridged tummy. A sun-kissed torso underneath swirls of thick, black chest hair.

She thought back to their initial meeting yesterday in her office when she'd wondered if the former wrestler still shaved his chest. She could put *that* question to rest.

She glanced at his head, hard and pink under the lights. "Your head…"

"What about it?"

"Do we have to go the Yul Brynner route?"

"Yul who?"

"The King and I?" As soon as she said it, she imagined herself in a satin gown, dancing in the arms of the King of Siam who, in this particular fantasy, looked like Nigel. *Although Nigel would never resort to the charming bullheadedness of the King. This guy is hopelessly sincere, and from what he mentioned about helping raise three kid sisters, dedicated.* She wasn't sure whether to be amused or amazed at this mass of man who had a body like The Rock and the heart of E.T.

Those baby blues had a confused look and she realized he still didn't get the Yul Brynner movie reference. "I think you should grow out your hair," she said, gesturing limply toward his fleshy dome. "Women like to run their fingers through a man's locks."

Nigel gave the dome a shake. "I can do the clothes, even try on a new name, but the head stays as is."

"Why?"

"Because I like it. No muss, no fuss."

"But women like to run their fingers—"

"Over my shiny bald scalp. After wrestling matches, I can't tell you how many fingers skimmed and rubbed and tickled the surface. Old women, young women, kids. Here, you do it." He leaned down, holding his head inches from her.

"This is ridiculous," she managed to say despite her pulse leaping into her throat.

"Feel it."

"I can see it."

"*Feel.*"

"If you had so many fingers feeling you—I mean, your head—why didn't you just hook up with…" It really wasn't any of her business why he hadn't latched on to one of the finger-feeling woman back in his Phantom days.

He glanced up, and something in his expression gave her heart a squeeze.

"Just 'cause they wanted to cop a feel didn't mean they wanted to know the real me."

She blinked, thinking how many women had complained about the exact same thing. Men just wanted them for their bodies, not their minds and heart. "You know, that's what a lot of women say about men."

He shrugged. "It's a curse and a blessing being a sensitive man."

She was wondering about the blessing part when he dropped his head, waiting for her to feel.

"Oh, no, that's all right—"

"I insist. Because afterward, you'll never ask me to grow my hair again."

"Okay," she whispered, reaching toward his scalp. She became aware of his scent—a citrusy aftershave. And she tried not to be overly aware that this mountain of a man, dressed in nothing but black stretchy briefs, was bending over in what looked like a bowing position.

For a moment, she felt like Anna taming the King of Siam.

And then her fingertips brushed lightly over his scalp, the connection warm, solid. She gasped and withdrew her fingers.

"No, touch me," Nigel insisted.

"I did," she said shakily.

He straightened a little, his blue eyes firing her a look. "That wasn't a touch." He gently took her hand and, bending down a little, placed it full on his bare scalp.

Her heart raced like a schoolgirl's as her palm pressed against his head, her fingers resting on smooth skin over hard skull. Back here, tucked away in a curtained room, pressing flesh to flesh, she suddenly felt as though they were doing something secretive, forbidden.

"It feels so…" She breathed in and out, her chest rising with the effort. "…silky, yet hard." She swallowed back a nervous sound, realizing how what she'd just said must sound.

Nigel still held her hand, his grip confident, warm. "Run your fingers over the surface," he said in a low voice that rumbled from deep within the mountain.

For a split second, she thought about lying and saying, oh, no, no, she'd felt enough, thank you. But in that blip of time, he started to guide her hand slowly, trailing her fingers in lazy paths over the sleek, pink dome.

"See?" he said, his voice low and husky. "It feels good, doesn't it?"

She murmured something in the affirmative, not trusting herself to form coherent words. The pounding of her heart had escalated to a pagan beat, pulsing loudly over the piped-in music.

Nigel straightened, slowly, causing her hand to slide ever so gently off his bare head and drift down the side of his face. Her fingers touched the bristle of his unshaven face.

As he straightened to his full height, her hand slid to his chest. She paused on the thick carpet of chest hair, feeling his heat through her fingertips.

After several long moments, as though awakening from a dream, she slowly withdrew her hand and stepped back through the curtain, her last image being the big, nearly naked man whose simmering blue eyes looked at her as though he'd discovered far more than she had in that sensual interlude.

3

Step two: Act like a bad boy

LATER THAT EVENING, Kimberly sat at the bar, sipping a diet cola, watching the front door. She'd told Nigel to meet her here at 7 p.m. so they could start step two, act like a bad boy, and here it was 7:20 and still no sign of him.

Of course, she'd gotten here only five minutes ago herself, but that was different. She was a one-woman corporation with responsibilities and meetings. Although, if she was perfectly honest with herself, she was developing some bad time-management habits. She used to occasionally run late in the mornings, but now she was late for almost every appointment. A few years ago, she had stayed on top of everything, juggling multiple responsibilities and never dropping one.

But these days...

She stirred the straw in her drink, thinking how the swirling ice cubes were like her life. Chunks of responsibilities, clattering against each other, going in circles. And she was jumping from cube to cube, trying to keep her balance, keep it all together.

"You want anything else?"

She looked up at the Tom Cruise look-alike bartender, reeking of testosterone and youth. Once upon a time, she'd fallen hard for that flavor of sultry, dark come-on. That's why she was so good at coaching men in the bad-boy department because she had ample firsthand experience.

"No, thank you."

He cocked an eyebrow, his mouth sliding in a half grin. "Alone?"

Stud Boy, test-drive it on someone else. "Temporarily."

"Aren't we all."

He turned, nodded to a customer flagging him down. "Need anything, let me know." He gave her a knowing wink.

Do I have Gone Without Sex Too Long tattooed on my forehead? She reached in her jacket pocket and extracted the half-eaten candy bar she'd been noshing on all day and took a bite.

A noise spread through the room. A light, suction-like sound.

She turned, dropping the bar into her pocket, realizing the sound was actually a series of gasps from clusters of women who were staring at the front door.

Kimberly followed their line of vision and froze.

There, filling the doorway, was a man bigger than life. Hercules in jeans and leather. He stood, taking his sweet time to scan the room, seemingly unaware that all eyes were on him. And although she prided herself on behaving professionally at all times, only a woman made of ice wouldn't have dropped her eyes to check out how such a man filled his jeans.

Full. Big.

As though she had X-ray vision, she recalled how he'd looked in those black stretchy briefs this afternoon.

"Nicky," Kimberly murmured under her breath, a spiral of heat curling within her. She dragged her gaze back up the jeans, over the tight baby-blue T-shirt she'd picked out because it matched the color his eyes, and the black leather jacket that masked him with a dark sensuality.

Damn, she knew how to dress a bad boy.

She quickly checked out the room, noticing how every woman had "pick me" written on her face.

Huffing in a lung-bursting prideful breath, Kimberly turned back in time to see Nigel waving energetically at her, a kidlike grin spreading the width of his face. With a gleeful burst of energy, he made a beeline for her, which was the first time she noticed he walked a bit pigeon-toed.

Bye-bye bad boy.

Releasing a sigh, Kimberly waved him over. *I definitely accomplished step one, look like a bad boy, but I have my work cut out for me with step two, act like one.*

The bar stool next to her creaked when he sat down.

"You're late," she said dryly.

"Didn't know punctuality was high on your list."

"I get busy."

"So do I." He flagged down the bartender and ordered a diet cola, slice of lime.

"No." Kimberly laid her hand on his, overly aware how big and warm it was. She flashed on touching his bald head this afternoon, how smooth and taut it had felt under her fingertips.

"No, what?" asked Nigel.

The bartender had arrived, a white bar towel tossed rakishly over his shoulder. His eyes glistened as he glanced at her hand on Nigel's before meeting her gaze.

She eased her hand back into her lap. "He'll have a beer."

The bartender cocked an eyebrow. His eyes not leaving hers, he asked, "Does he have a preference for what kind?"

"No," growled Nigel. "He doesn't."

The bartender nodded curtly, flashing Nigel a whipped look as he sauntered away.

"Oh, yeah, I look like a real bad boy with you correcting my order."

"This is a coaching session, not a date."

"Just curious, coach, when was the last time you went on a date?"

She hesitated, debating whether to feel affronted by the question, even as her mind reeled back to a year ago. She'd met the guy—who said he did radio and TV marketing—at a coffee shop, and he'd spontaneously asked her out to lunch. She, who never did anything spur of the moment, had said yes.

Fifteen minutes later, when their sandwiches arrived, she regretted her moment of spontaneity. The guy was fidgety, jumping from topic to topic barely taking a break for breathing. During a topic shift she excused herself from the table "to take a call" and kept walking all the way out to the street, to her car, and she drove back to work.

"My dating history isn't important." *Is Has No Social Life also tattooed on my forehead?* "This is about you, not me."

"I've upset you."

Yes. "No."

"Sorry."

"No problem." She fumbled in her pocket for the candy bar. Peeling off the wrapping, she tossed the last bite into her mouth. Squeezing the paper into a tight ball, she set it in a nearby ashtray.

"What'd you have to eat today?"

"I need to coach you on acting like a bad boy," she said, her mouth still full.

Nigel folded his arms, the leather crinkling with the movement. "You should at least eat a nutritional breakfast. If you're in a hurry, nuke some oatmeal, toss in some raisins. Wash it down with a glass of skim milk and you've covered three of your four food groups right there."

"Oh, are there four?" she said, feeling petty and tired of being the focus of recent quasi nutritionists. Between him and Maurice, a woman couldn't pop anything into her mouth. She didn't dare tell Nigel that up to a month ago she had smoked.

The bartender plunked down the beer in front of Nigel. "Added your lime," he said.

"Thanks." Nigel plucked the slice of lime from the mouth of the bottle and squeezed some of the juice into the drink.

Taking a long swig of the beer, Nigel thought back to how Kimberly said she'd never watched cartoons growing up and it hit him how this woman had probably never been a little girl. No wonder she wore these strange clothes and ate sugar nonstop. It was as though no one had ever coached *her* on how to take care of herself, be comfortable in her own skin.

"Okay," she said, her face taking on that pinched expression when she was about to say something serious. "Let's talk about acting like a bad boy."

He nodded, noticing how a wisp of her hair had escaped her bun. It looked pretty and wild the way it fell against her cheek.

"First and foremost," she said, "bad boys are superconfident, cool. I'd like you to check out some movies like *The Wild One* with Marlon Brando or *Don Juan DeMarco* with Johnny Depp." She glanced at his head. "I've also heard movies with someone named Vin Diesel are good, too."

Vin Diesel? From some of the movie trailers he'd seen, that actor made bad look downright evil. "You're the coach," he murmured before taking another swig of beer.

"Don't come on heavy, keep it light. And never touch a woman first. Let her do all the touching."

"I already do that."

She blinked. "Right. Well, good. You're a step ahead on the road to bad boy." She cleared her throat. "Let's now talk about pick-up lines. Don't use cliché ones like 'Do you know CPR because you take my breath away.' Or 'I lost my phone number. Can I have yours?' Stuff like that. Trust me, women have heard them all."

"I've never, nor will ever, use those." He shifted closer, catching a whiff of that hothouse orchid perfume again. "How's this?" Lowering his voice, he whispered, "You look a little skinny. Can I bake you a batch of brownies?"

Kimberly blinked. "No."

"Chocolate chip cookies?"

"No, no baking lines." She frowned. "Although the skinny comment was good." A slight smile, almost unnoticeable, touched her lips.

Nigel wondered if she ever really smiled. Not something manufactured or halfway, but a real genuine one.

"Your best bet is to simply compliment a woman, and I do mean simply. Keep it honest, keep it short. A few words on her looks. Or something she's wearing. Even a piece of jewelry. Then say nothing."

"Honest, short compliments."

"Exactly." She turned away from him, staring at the bottles of alcohol lined up at the back of the bar. "Okay, I'm Jane Doe, sitting here, minding my own business. Practice on me."

He looked at her profile, noticing a slight bump on the bridge of her nose. A childhood accident? Definitely not something to compliment her on. His gaze dropped to her lips, pretty and full and still slicked with the blood-red lipstick. *Let me muss your lipstick?* No, that wasn't a compliment.

He looked again at that wisp of errant hair that glinted gold under the light. He leaned forward. "You have beautiful hair," he said in a low, throaty voice. "The color of sunshine."

She nodded slightly, barely glancing at him. "Yes, yes, that's good. Try another."

He leaned closer, easing in a lungful of that hothouse perfume. "If I were your man," he whispered hotly into her ear, "I'd make sure you were wearing both earrings before you left the house."

She shuddered a release of breath. Then, as his words registered, she straightened and touched one earlobe, then the other.

"Oh!" she exclaimed, touching the bare lobe. "I forgot to put one on."

Folding her hands demurely in her lap, she swiveled on the stool and looked directly at him. "All right," she said, rolling back her shoulders. "You seem to have a handle on one-liners. Just stay away from cooking references. And, by the way, when you enter a bar, no grinning and waving."

"Huh?"

"Like what you did when you walked into the bar a few minutes ago."

"What am I supposed to do?"

"You started out right. Self-confident, cool. You paused in the doorway and slowly scanned the room. At that moment, every woman's eyes were on you, hoping she'd be the one. We'll go to another bar in a few minutes, practice your entrance... Oh, one more thing. Are you...a bit pigeon-toed?"

"When I walk too fast." She was more eagle-eyed than the nuns at Catholic school.

"Slow down, then. And before we leave, let's practice how you sit at a bar."

He looked down. "What's wrong with this?"

"You look...perched. Like a bald eagle on a branch." She darted a look at his head. "Sorry."

Actually, it was a bit funny even though she didn't seem to think so. "No offense taken. What kind of animal should I be?"

She paused, then snapped her fingers. "A panther. Sleek, powerful, sensual. And instead of sitting, lean seductively against the bar."

He frowned. "Seductively?"

"Just lean your hip against the bar. Trust me, it'll look hot and bad. Go ahead, try it."

He stood and pressed a hip against the bar.

She tilted her head. "Can you slouch a little? Your hip looks attached to the bar."

He bent one knee. "Like this?"

"No, no. Watch me." In one smooth motion, she slid off her stool and thrust one hip against the bar. Leaning back a little, she planted an elbow on the bar while sliding an "I'm here, check me out" look across the bar.

Nigel was spellbound. He'd wondered before where she kept her passion and right now he saw it in action. In that one liquid move, she'd confirmed the old saying, "You can't judge a book by its cover."

"See what I mean?"

"Oh, yeah." His blood was heating up, racing to his groin.

She straightened. "Now, you try it."

"Uh, I'm tired of practicing here. Let's head to the next bar, practice there."

She pursed her lips, looking perplexed. "I want to be a good coach—"

"Trust me," he rasped, stealing her line, "you are." He downed another sip of beer, willing the rush of cold to temper his boiling blood.

NIGEL STOOD OUTSIDE THE BAR, a place called Scarlett's on the outskirts of Vegas away from the hustle of the strip. He wondered how Kimberly picked these places—she seemed too straitlaced to go to them herself.

He inhaled the evening air, grateful as always this time of year not to be in his hometown of Boston where February could be brutal. Unlike Vegas where February was sweet, easy. Like early spring. Balmy, the air touched with scents of jasmine and orange.

He glanced up at the neon sign over the door of the bar. A thin red light flashed along the outline of a woman in a hoop dress. He thought about Kimberly's red suit and wondered if she ever wore something soft and flouncy. If she ever reveled in her femininity.

His gut told him no.

What a waste of woman.

From helping raise his kid sisters, Nigel had seen firsthand how a girl flowered into a woman. Each of his sisters was different, and yet each had the same need to feel special, be listened to, know that she was appealing to the opposite sex. And in the course of evolving into a woman, each developed her own individual tastes and values.

He pondered what Kimberly valued.

Money, he guessed, was top of the list.

A distant second might be…jelly beans.

Nigel chuckled to himself. Jelly beans. Candy bars. God bless that Maurice fellow for sneaking in an occasional breakfast burrito. Yesterday, watching the exchange between Maurice and Kimberly was priceless—she obviously didn't approve of her assistant's meddling and he didn't give a hoot what she thought.

That had to be the key to getting through Ms. Logan's uptight persona. Like the saying in that ad, Just Do It.

Hey, maybe he could take this game a step further. Not just try out some stances and lines, but get through to her. If he could shake loose some of Ms. Logan's frosty exterior, just imagine the power he'd have with other women!

Yeah, he'd wrap up this second step fast, move on to whatever three was. Something about melting women. The sooner he got through these steps, the sooner he'd find true love.

Nigel stepped up to the door, placed his hand on the brass knob, ready to be Nicky, the baddest of the bad.

The bar was darker, moodier than the other one. True to its name, Scarlett's, pinpoints of red light punctured the smoky atmosphere. An old Tony Bennett tune threaded the air, the deep melodious voice crooning about his solitude and being haunted by the memories of a woman.

He shut the door behind him and stood for a moment absorbing the sights and sounds in the room. Glasses clinked. Tony crooned. At some tables, he saw huddled forms. In the corner, next to a jukebox, a couple danced. To the far left was the bar, its track lighting reflected in a mirror that ran the length of the wall behind it. Several people sat on stools nursing drinks, some chatting, some alone.

And then he saw her.

Kimberly sat in the corner seat against the wall. Light spilled down her, making that red suit glow like fire. Except for her red lips, the rest of her face was in shadow. She was watching him, her body still except for her hand gently swirling a straw in her drink.

The way she'd positioned herself, most of her face masked in shadow, reminded him of an animal observing its prey. She in the dark, he in the light. Oh, yes, Ms. Logan thrived on being in the driver's seat, controlling the situation, and suddenly he wanted nothing better than to shake up her world.

Beat her at her own game.

Ms. Logan, he thought as he started to shrug off his jacket, *before the night is over I'm going to get under your skin. This bad boy isn't going to just "practice" on you. He's going to unleash some of your tightly bottled passion.*

He stepped forward, mindful not to walk too fast so he didn't lapse into that slightly pigeon-toed walk. He eased into a shaft of red light, shrugging the rest of the way out of his jacket, flexing a bicep as he slung the jacket over his shoulder.

Tony crooned about how, in his solitude, a woman taunted him....

Taunt her.

Nigel purposefully—*slowly*—strolled away from the part of the bar where Kimberly sat. He headed to the opposite side where he straddled a bar stool—something she hadn't coached him in but he remembered some badass actor doing it in a chick flick his sisters had loved. Sitting, Nigel ignored Kimberly, resting one elbow on the bar as he cruised the room with his gaze.

A thirtysomething woman sat alone a few seats from him. Her auburn hair fell stylishly to her shoulders, her makeup bright. What gave away her profession was the see-through blouse unbuttoned to reveal a teasing glimpse of cleavage.

He moved on.

At a nearby table sat two middle-aged women, the

kind Nigel had seen plenty of in the eight years he'd made Vegas his home. Perennially tanned, toned, their hair a shade of champagne-blond that looked like neither. One of them stared at him, and he offered a slight nod of his head. She smiled, pleased for the attention.

He moved on.

After scouring the room, he turned back and eased his gaze to the corner where he met Kimberly's shadowed eyes. She was holding the straw, no longer stirring. Was she surprised he hadn't made a beeline for her? Did she wonder why he'd chosen to sit at the far end of the bar, away from her?

Good. He'd thrown her off.

"What'll it be, pal?" The bartender pushed a coaster in front of Nigel.

"Whisky. Neat." That should shake her up even more. Screw cold beer. He wanted something with a bite.

The bartender set a glass on the coaster, held up a bottle of amber liquid for Nigel's approval. He nodded, then watched over the guy's shoulder as he poured.

Kimberly's posture had straightened, as though on alert. When she moved forward slightly, light fell across her face. Under the splash of light, he noticed how when she looked surprised her eyes were almost too big for her face.

She looked curious. No, *curious* was too simple a word. He thought back to how she'd snapped that pencil in two. This lady's emotions ran deep, were complex. And she hadn't gotten to where she was without a healthy dose of self-centeredness.

She looked *apprehensive*. Undoubtedly worried what Nigel had ordered, and why.

Move over honey. You're no longer in the driver's seat.

Pleased with himself, Nigel slid the bartender a ten and told him to keep the change. He raised the glass to his lips but didn't drink. He held it there, savoring the heady aroma, the scent triggering memories of Kimberly's perfume. Did it grow stronger the closer a man got to it? When aroused, did the heat of her skin add a pungent, exotic twist to the flowery scent?

He took a sip, savoring its sting while boldly holding her gaze.

She pressed her hands together, shifted a little in her seat.

He sensed the tug between them, even while telling himself this was a contrived encounter, a silly game. Yet his radar told him they both felt something more. Something primal and needy that sharpened his need to best her.

To have her.

When she dabbed a nervous tongue on her lip, he made his move.

He grabbed his jacket and slid off the seat. Then he ambled past the woman with auburn hair, all the way around the bar to where Kimberly sat.

He tossed his jacket on the bar and stood in front of her.

She looked up, those big eyes wet, luminous. Her lips parted as though to speak, but instead she fluttered her fingers to the top button on her prim blouse.

Nigel shifted closer, watching her mouth go slack. His knee brushed hers, the accidental touch triggering small fires over his skin.

From the rising flush in her cheeks, she felt it, too. Her fingers dropped to the single button on her jacket. She undid it, pulling back the jacket as though to cool herself.

He slouched against the bar, liking the shift in control.

As a small concession to her rules, he rested his elbow on the bar top, just as she'd shown him, and dutifully scanned the room again.

Tony was still crooning. Glasses clinked. A woman laughed somewhere in the shadows. Everything was the same as when he'd first walked in here.

But since he'd entered this room, something inside of him had changed. He'd walked in here to play a game—a game that was suddenly feeling all too real.

He looked back at Kimberly.

She was studying him…and he swore he saw her heart in her eyes. He could have left it at this—an off-balance moment soldered with heat and unspoken desire, but that look in her eyes darkened.

And when those too-red, too-perfect lips whispered, "Please," with an aching sweetness, a blast of fire shot straight through him.

The moment slid into something primitive and out of control.

He leaned forward and whispered hotly into her ear, "I want you."

He heard her gasp. From the corner of his eye, saw her breasts heave underneath the filmy silk blouse.

And in a moment of liquid heat, he slid one arm around her waist and pulled her to him, feeling her swollen breasts against his body. She shivered, her breath escaping in a low moan.

"We shouldn't—"

But his lips were on hers, devouring the rest of her words.

4

SHE TASTED SWEET AND HOT. He teased the soft under-cushion of her lip with his tongue. She shivered, hesitated, then leaned forward and returned his kiss.

Lips so soft, moist, pliable. He could consume her right here and now, starting with this mouth and working his way through the rest of her body. He could almost taste her essence, smell pockets of that exotic perfume, feel the liquid movements of her skin against his....

She pulled back slightly, gasped a small breath.

He pressed his palm against the bar, bracing himself against doing more. He'd moved too fast, acted without thinking. Part of him had touched on his old Phantom persona, acting willful and demanding, going after the win. A side he'd never used with women—not in his real life, anyway—although women professed to want just that in the volume of fan mail he'd received when that damn commercial aired. Some of his pals had kidded him, saying he was a fool to not go after a sure thing. But he'd already tasted the life of being admired and bedded for being The Phantom. Nothing felt more hollow than waking up with a stranger who wants you for someone you're not.

And, ironically, here he was doing it again. Pretending to be someone he wasn't to get someone to love him for who he really was.

Too damn complicated. Can't play the game again.

Nigel raised his head to say as much, but when he caught Kimberly's sleepy look, those velvet-gray eyes glistening with need, all thoughts shot straight out of his head.

"Kimberly, you're...so...beautiful."

Surprise, then pleasure flickered across her face, making him wonder when a man had last complimented her. Make that *dared* to compliment her. The lady had a formidable presence, although she'd undermined that by wearing a fire-engine red suit.

His gaze dropped to those matching fire-engine red lips.

They were swollen, the crimson finally smeared.

A little imperfection did the woman good—gave her a deliciously sexy edge. One thing he'd learned in the ring, the world abhors perfection. Audiences pay big bucks not only to see a wrestler's Achilles' heel, but his or her struggle, even failure, because of it. Because an audience's love was born of flames. But just as they hungered to see you fall to your knees, they roared their approval if you crawled back from the ashes, bleeding and scarred, and hurled yourself triumphant back into the game.

Because if you could crash through barriers, over-come horrific odds, people believed they could, too.

A weight lodged in his chest as he saw the van-quished warrior in Kimberly. She might look and act like a general in her uptight suits and take-no-prisoners attitude, but she was still crawling back from some battle, scarred and damaged. Unlike The Phantom and his experience in the ring, she had no one cheering her on as she hurled herself back into the game.

He rubbed the pad of his thumb across a patch of her unbearably soft cheek. As much as he wanted to console her, he wanted even more to take her into his arms and make slow, lingering love to her.

"Nicky," she whispered.

"Nigel," he corrected huskily.

"You…weren't supposed to come on heavy." She made a movement as though to pull away, but didn't.

He paused, almost withdrew his hand, but couldn't. He liked being close to her, liked how her face felt so warm, so soft in his hands. Liked how that wayward wisp of hair tickled his skin.

Liked being the man in her life, taking care of her even if it was only for this moment.

"You're not supposed to touch first…"

The look in her eyes made her a liar. This was a woman who hadn't been touched in too long.

"You have more rules about what not to do," he murmured, "than what to do…."

Kimberly shuddered with anticipation as his

mouth drew near. His masculine scent—soapy, tinged with that citrusy aftershave—shot straight to her brain, infusing every brain cell.

Almost every.

Some distant corner of her mind, like a star in a faraway galaxy, flashed a warning she shouldn't be doing this. This was supposed to be business, not pleasure. She had her reputation to uphold, something she'd worked hard to rebuild after it'd been shredded to nothing in another town, another lifetime ago....

But this close to his heat, her internal warnings faded, replaced by a constellation of feelings and needs that seared white-hot through her. She leaned forward, falling toward him like a planet succumbing to the intense pull of a dark star.

And how she wanted to fall.

He shifted his weight, tilted his head, and she caught flecks of gold in those impossibly blue eyes. For an intense, surreal moment, their gazes held as the world receded away, as far away as that remote star, leaving only her and Nigel in their own corner of the universe.

His stare, filled with that same knowing look he'd given her earlier in the dressing room, filled her with a delicious, hot ache. Nobody had looked at her like that in years.

His lips touched hers. Lips that were hot and hard, like his body. He paused, his mouth barely touching hers as he murmured something sweet, barely audible, against her lips.

Then he kissed her.

A small fear held her in check. Fear of him, fear of herself letting go. Feelings overridden by other hot, urgent ones as he claimed her mouth, and she willfully, greedily returned his kiss like a child craving food and drink.

With other men, it had always been easy to assess their tension or awkwardness and fall into her familiar, controlling role and put an end to it. Some men had reacted defensively, or even crudely, and she'd always handled it as she might a business deal gone awry. Professionally, coolly, like a queen not wishing to be bothered with a gnat.

Sometimes, afterward, she'd wonder if she'd permanently closed herself off to experiencing intimacy again. But her self-analysis never lasted long. She'd made it a personal rule to never dwell and wonder "what if" as she'd once done, as though mulling a problem to death had the power to heal one's life.

At this moment, however, with this man, she suddenly realized that those past experiences with men had been fraught with confusion and awkwardness because they hadn't felt right.

Kissing Nigel felt right.

So right, it was terrifying.

With a gasp, she pulled back. The world swirled around her, gradually rocking into place. Slowly her senses adjusted to the moodily lighted bar, the clink of bar glasses.

"I can't," she whispered.

Nigel paused, blinked like a man awoken from a deep slumber. "Can't?" He gave his head a shake. "Why?"

"You're—" *so right* "—my client."

He played with a tendril of her hair, the wisp of gold falling over and over his big brown fingers. "Maybe I've graduated, and this is no longer a business relationship."

She slid a glance at the bartender, who discreetly looked away as he wiped a glass with a dish towel. Across the bar, she met a stranger's stare, his dark eyes glittering not so discreetly.

She looked quickly back into Nigel's eyes.

"I think," she murmured, struggling to regain control, "that you've successfully accomplished step two."

He frowned. "And that was…?"

"Act like a bad boy," she rasped, absently pulling her jacket closed and buttoning it as though that tidied up whatever had just happened between them.

"Was it an act?" He released the strand of hair, dropped his hand onto the bar.

She paused, surprised at his comeback. Where was the big mountain of mellow man she'd met only yesterday? The one with that rooster cartoon character on his T-shirt, the man who damn near swooned when she put on Celine Dion? Either she'd outdone herself in her clothing-makeover zeal, or this man had one hell of an inner bad boy thundering to the forefront.

He cocked an eyebrow, waiting for her answer.

"Beats me," she admitted. "Want a refund?"

His half smile dissolved. "No. You're good for me."

She nodded as though agreeing with him, feeling clueless how she could be good for him considering she'd just lost her head. She'd never behaved this way with a client. She'd never even *flirted* with a client despite provocation from some who decided they'd rather be successful with their success coach than to keep pounding the singles' turf.

"I'm not good for you," she murmured, avoiding Nigel's eyes. "Not in that way." She fumbled to retrieve several bills from her purse. She wished she hadn't stopped smoking. Right now a long, hard draw on a cigarette would calm her heat-singed nerves.

He touched her arm. "I still want…to work with you."

"I've betrayed our business agreement by crossing the line."

He stared at her, frowned. "So move the line. It's imaginary, right?"

She laid a bill on the counter and picked up her drink. Damn, her hand was shaking. She took a quick, cool sip, set the sweating glass back down and cleared her throat. "I can recommend you to another agency. They're quite good, and your contract with Life Dates can be transferred to them." She flagged down the bartender.

Nigel leaned close, his breath feathering hot against her ear. "Why are you being difficult?"

Fighting to keep her composure, she indicated to the bartender to give her back three dollars. As he walked away, she slid a look at Nigel. "Just because I'm difficult doesn't mean I'm not right. This is a business relationship, not a—" She paused, the words sticking in her throat.

"Not a what?"

"Let me put it this way. I'll never get married again. Ever. So what's the use?"

For a long, wordless moment, their gazes held. She'd surprised him with her outburst. And it wasn't her pride that made her realize she'd disappointed him, too. She could see it in his eyes, those beautiful, tender blue eyes. Remorse shot through her, sharp as a knife, and for an instant she doubted everything she'd ever thought or felt or learned. Because in some deep, sixth-sense way she knew, *knew,* this man would stand by her through the good and the bad, love her until she drew her last breath. If she were coaching Kimberly Logan, she'd call the woman a crazy fool to pass up the very thing it took so many others a lifetime to find.

She opened her mouth to speak, madly juggling her thoughts, unsure how much or what to say, but needing to express *something.*

"Gotta go," he said gruffly, muttering something under his breath about regimented, uptight women.

"Nicky, I—"

"Nigel." He picked up his jacket. "That's our problem. You want me to be somebody else."

And with that, he turned and left.

Kimberly watched him walk away, observed how the overhead red lights rippled over his form, witnessed women's heads turning, men looking startled or envious.

The front door shut solidly behind him.

She put her wallet back into her purse, told herself that gutted feeling would pass. Time to go home, prepare for the advertising agency meeting next week.

As she exited the bar and stepped into the balmy night air, she reminded herself she'd been right.

Even though a small voice inside kept whispering she'd been wrong, so wrong.

THIRTY MINUTES LATER, Nigel's front doorbell rang.

He frowned, checked the wall clock. Ten-thirty? Who'd be showing up this time of night?

He opened the door and his heart thudded wildly.

Kimberly.

She gave him a sheepish look before her gaze shifted to his bare chest.

"I was getting ready for bed," he mumbled, explaining why he only had on his jeans.

She looked back up. Even in the muted glow of the porch light, he saw her blush.

She cleared her throat. "Sorry to bother you," she said, gesturing aimlessly. "I dropped by the office, looked up your address. Which I've never done before—unless there's been an emergency—but this, well, felt like an emergency." She released a weighty sigh. "I want to apologize for how I behaved."

"For kissing me?"

"No, no, well maybe, yes, but—" she cleared her throat again "—for overreacting to the situation. I could have handled it better, not acted so—"

"No need to apologize."

A breeze gusted past, bringing a scent of honeysuckle. In the distance, an owl hooted.

"Want a glass of lemonade?" asked Nigel.

She blinked. "No, I should go."

But she didn't.

Impulsively, he reached out and took her hand. It felt small, soft. "You worry too much," he murmured, tugging gently.

She stepped inside and looked around. His place looked supersize. An overstuffed leather chair, a couch that could surely sit six, a plant in the corner that should be paying half the mortgage.

He gestured to the couch. "Have a seat, I'll be right back."

He returned with two glasses of lemonade and handed her one, then sat at the far end of the couch. It was better here, in the brightly lit comfort of his home, than in the moody lighting of the bar. Seeing her clearly, he grew acutely aware of their differences. His skin bronzed from the sun, hers fair from staying indoors. His body large, muscles layered over a broad-shouldered frame. Hers, slender with soft curves.

Differences, yes, but complementary. The way it should be between a man and a woman.

He took a quick sip, welcoming the jolt of cold liquid. He didn't want to think about the whole man-woman thing because he'd just let down his guard again. She'd made it clear at the bar that there was a line between them, and he was to stay on his side.

"You have a lot of photos," she said, looking around the room.

"My family."

"Large."

"And then some. Three siblings, seven aunts and uncles, more cousins than I can count. Most still live in my hometown, Boston."

"My family stayed in my hometown, too." She set her glass on the coffee table. "A dad and a brother."

He heard regret in her voice. Instinctively, he shifted closer. "Miss them?"

She shrugged. "I miss…what used to be. Not how it was when I left." She laughed, a sharp sound. "Let's just say I rode out of town on a black horse, not a white one. I'll never be the dirty joke of my community again. I learned the hard way that creating and maintaining a respectable reputation is critical to success."

Dirty joke? He'd have pegged Kimberly Logan, president and businesswoman extraordinaire, as many things in her past—a straight-A student, state champion baton twirler—anything but a dirty joke. No wonder she was so guarded. She was determined to protect herself at all costs.

"You're safe with me." The words came out unexpectedly, but as soon as he said them, he knew what she needed. A sanctuary.

For a moment he caught a glimpse of vulnerability in her eyes. Then she surprised him with a soft, startled laugh as she reached out and touched his arm.

"I know," she whispered.

The moment hung suspended between them, her touch searing right through his skin and turning his insides molten.

He realized he was gripping his damn lemonade so hard, he might crush the glass with his bare hand. Releasing a whoosh of pent-up breath, he set it down on the table.

"I think it's time you left," he murmured.

"Did I say something wrong?"

He lowered his eyes to her lips and swallowed, hard. Suddenly, he stood, keeping his back to her. Best not to face her considering these damn bad-boy jeans, which were already too tight, were ready to burst at the seams thanks to his roaring hard-on.

"What did I do?" she asked.

"Nothing," he croaked.

And he probably could have pulled off the painfully noble act if he didn't feel her soft, tentative touch on his back. He closed his eyes, swearing he didn't sense her body heat, didn't catch an intoxicating whiff of that hothouse perfume.

"Nigel," she whispered, gently pulling on his arm, beckoning him to turn and face her.

In the ring, he could strong-arm a three-hundred-pound opponent, but at this moment he was putty with a one-hundred-pound-plus woman. Like a doomed man, he turned and looked down into her face. Those gray eyes glittered with concern, her curvaceous lips parting slightly as she seemed to ponder what to say.

Damn if he wasn't holding his breath, terrified to move, not wanting to say or do the wrong thing.

"The line," he finally murmured.

"What?"

"You're crossing it."

Her pulse throbbed in her throat. She closed her eyes, slowly, then reopened them, giving him a look that made his breath burn in his chest.

"Damn the line," she murmured.

That did it. He cupped the back of her neck and lowered his mouth to hers. A bolt of shock and pleasure ricocheted through his body as she parted her lips with a soft groan.

She tasted like lemons and summer, tangy and hot. He stroked her lips with his tongue before plunging into the moist heat of her mouth, sucking on her tongue, craving more with each suction and release.

She reared back her head and gasped, then gripped his head and tugged him back for more. Her return kiss was primal, wanton, her nimble tongue seeking, exploring every corner of his mouth.

He splayed one hand against her back and tugged her closer, growling with pleasure as her body molded to his. He felt starved, the empty years furiously catching up with him. He tunneled his fingers into her hair, grounding her in place as his lips drove into hers, urgently, frantically making up for lost time. As their tongues curled and coiled in a desperate mating dance, he was aware of nails digging into his back, the incinerating heat of her mouth, their passion escalating to an intolerable urgency.

He could take her right here. Rip off those pants, bend her over the couch and bury himself into her.

He broke away, his chest heaving with ragged pants.

After a beat, he cradled her face, a silent apology if he'd been too rough, too uncontrolled.

She took his hand, kissed it. Without breaking eye contact, she released his hold and plucked open the button of her jacket. Removing it, she let it drop to the floor, followed by her blouse. She started to unsnap the clasp on the front of her bra, no more than a wisp of pink, when he reached out and gently took her hands.

"My turn," he murmured.

He laid her hands at her sides, then opened the clasp and peeled back the gauzy material to expose her breasts. Round and pink tipped, they puckered at the onslaught of cool air.

"Lovely," he growled.

He traced a tightening circle around one breast, then the other, lightly tugging on a pebbled nipple.

Kimberly gasped with pleasure and reached for his belt. He again caught her hands.

"Tonight," he said gruffly, "I'm *your* success coach."

She started to speak, paused, then smiled slyly.

"Good," he said, returning her smile. "Because I'm afraid I'm a bit, uh, unprepared." He shrugged, squeezed her hands. "Wasn't expecting company. Actually, haven't had any reason to be prepared for a long time, if you get my drift."

"I get it," she said softly. "Me, too."

Kimberly felt momentarily stunned by this powerful hulk of a man's sincerity. Words didn't come lightly to him. If he gave his, he kept it. And she knew instinctually it was the same with his heart. If he gave it, there were no strings, no games. His love was unadulterated. Innocent, even.

Something in her chest constricted and she told herself it wasn't her heart. *I can't fall in love with this man.*

Yet she could hardly breathe for the way he was looking at her, the blue of his eyes darkening, his mouth softening. He leaned over and kissed her again, his lips consuming hers with such restrained lust and open tenderness, her heart ached with longing.

Without saying a word, he gently finished undressing her. Across the room, she caught their reflection in a sliding-glass door. She stood, naked and pale. He knelt before her, his massive, bronzed back bending to her will. When he slid his hands between her thighs and gently prodded them apart, she willingly obeyed, ready to shed her defenses and be vulnerable to him, greedy for herself.

His hands moved up, trailing fire across her sensitive skin until he reached her sex.

He opened her and blew softly.

She shuddered, gripped his shoulders.

His tongue flicked her, *there*.

She gasped, her knees nearly buckling.

"I got you," he murmured, getting a firm hold on her hips.

Her thoughts shattered as he again found her sensitive nub and suckled.

Her body rigid with excitement, her breaths coming in pants, she looked down at his head moving between her legs, felt his taut shoulder muscles underneath her hands, listened to his guttural sounds of pleasure, and thought this had to be the most erotic moment she'd ever experienced in her life.

As desire pooled hot between her legs, she dropped back her head and succumbed to the delicious sensations of nibbling, sucking, licking. His mouth was so mobile, so skilled.

Heat and need consumed her, drove her as her hips undulated lightly, uncontrollably, against his laving tongue. She wanted more, needed more....

As his tongue swirled around and around, sucking deep, her insides suddenly convulsed. Sensation deep within her peaked and hung suspended for an excruciating moment....

"Nigel," she suddenly cried out.

Her first climax ripped through her as a ragged moan of release escaped her lips. Then she rode wave after wave of release, her body, mind and soul melding into one hot, pulsating mass until finally, satiated down to her toes, she fell limply against him.

"Beautiful," he murmured, taking one last taste before trailing light kisses along her stomach, breasts, face as he rose. Then he lifted her onto the couch and cradled her in his arms.

They sat quietly this way for a long time, her head on his chest as she listened to the soft thud of his heartbeat. Being close like this in the aftermath of intimacy, she felt more vulnerable than ever.

Uncomfortably so.

In a heated moment, she'd told herself it was all right to cross the line, but what she hadn't fully realized was the line wasn't *between* them, but *within* her. She'd exposed more of herself than she'd wanted and she feared if she didn't go back, close off, she'd lose herself.

She slowly extracted herself from his hold and stood.

Leaning over, she started picking up her clothes. "I have to go home now," she murmured.

THE NEXT MORNING, Nigel was laying out some paint chips in the kitchen to show his best buddy Rigo. If Nigel had his way, he'd be at Life Dates right now, interrogating Kimberly on her disappearing act last night, but that would have to wait until after Rigo left.

"Man, I'm not saying you're wrong, just that, well, royal plum seems…" Rigo crossed his arms, the bulging brown muscles obliterating the WrestleMania logo on his tank top, a reminder of the days when he and Nigel had been opponents in the wrestling ring. Rigo the Wrecker versus The Phantom. Onstage their antics had been brutal and vicious, but offstage they'd been best pals. Still were.

Rigo rubbed a thumb along his full bottom lip, eyeing Nigel's kitchen, which he was in the process of remodeling. Brightly colored paint chips lay amid samples of wallpaper and fabric swatches on the old butcher-block kitchen table. The scent of beef stew filled the air. A portable radio, propped on a corner of the wood and marble kitchen counter Nigel had recently installed, was tuned to Star Moods, a New Age program that played planetarium music. Nigel still wasn't sure what planetarium music was, but he liked its soothing tunes.

"Royal plum seems...?" prompted Nigel, scratching Renée, Rigo's wife's miniature white poodle, behind the ears. Just as Rigo had once been the Wrecker on stage, he'd also been the wrecker of women's hearts offstage. Until he met Lydia, a gregarious Pilates instructor who also ran an increasingly profitable business on E-Bay selling hand-embroidered handbags. Working at home would be a plus when their first baby, due in two months, was born.

Rigo blew out a breath. "Just seems over the top, man."

Nigel smiled, knowing "over the top" meant unmacho to Rigo.

This was not the moment to kid Rigo that walking a pint-size poodle named Renée might be construed as "over the top," too.

Nigel looked at the paint chip, thinking how this rich purple complemented Kimberly's soft gray eyes. He tossed the chip aside, wishing he'd stop thinking about her.

"Why not paint your kitchen white like everybody else?" asked Rigo.

"White?" Nigel did a dramatic double take, a move reminiscent of their days in the ring. "That's the *1980s,* brother. We're in the twenty-first millennium, where it's manly to add splashes of color."

Rigo's dark eyes sparkled with amusement as he looked around the in-progress kitchen. "What's that style you're doin' again?"

"Country. Well, mostly."

Nigel knew his friend didn't give a shit if a kitchen style was country, traditional or out-of-this-world alien. As long as the refrigerator had an automatic ice maker, and the stove turned on, that was a good enough style for him.

Renée, staring intently up into Rigo's face, suddenly yapped twice.

"I just fed you," he argued with the dog.

Renée sidled up to Rigo's size-thirteen foot, laid her fuzzy white head on it and gave him a woe-is-me look.

"Women," Rigo muttered. "Nige, care to offer a starving lady a bite of stew?"

"Sure." When Rigo had been a bachelor, he'd sworn he'd never put a ring on any woman's finger, especially a woman who owned one of those "rats on a string." But Lydia and Renée, her poodle—named after Lydia's favorite actress Renée Zellweger—had been a package deal.

The next thing Nigel knew, Rigo the perennial stud morphed into Rigo the eternally smitten. One of the proudest moments of Nigel's life was standing next to Rigo as his best man at Lydia and Rigo's wedding a year ago.

Nigel spooned a ladle of the stew into a small bowl, which he placed in the freezer for a moment to cool it down. "What's Lydia doing tonight?"

"Girls' night out. She thinks it'll be her last one for a while."

"Picked a baby's name yet?"

Rigo shrugged. "Lydia wants to name her Nicole."

"Don't tell me."

"Yeah, after that movie star. The one who was married to Tom what's-his-face. You know how Lydia loves her movies."

Nigel laughed. "Brother, I foresee you and a houseful of women. Let's see—" he counted off on his fingers "—there'll be little Nicole, little JLo, little Catherine Zeta—"

Rigo faked putting Nigel into a headlock, which Nigel countered with a feigned move called the Stunner. Renée ran in circles, barking. After a few minutes, the two men broke apart, laughing.

Nigel opened the freezer door. "You're holding up okay for an old man."

"Yeah, you're not bad yourself for being over the hill."

"Younger than you."

"By not much."

Nigel took out the bowl. "Five years."

"Two."

"Oh, right, two. You just *look* a lot older."

Rigo laughed as Nigel poured some of the sauce into the sink, then set the offering on the floor. Renée approached the bowl cautiously, then walked around it in a semicircle, sniffing its contents.

"Thought she was hungry," said Nigel. He leaned his hip against the counter, watching the dog. "Reminds me of my dating days. It's all part of the dance."

With a soft woof, Renée began chowing down.

"Yeah," Rigo continued drolly, "that reminds me of my dating days, too. Some women act all detached and sweet, but later you discover they have voracious appetites. Speaking of dating days, how's yours?"

Nigel thought back to his sizzling encounter with Kimberly last night, wishing he knew what the hell happened. Her hasty exit was akin to being clotheslined over the top rope before the match barely started.

Why even think about it? We have nothing in common.
He was laid-back, she was uptight. He wanted a

family, she wanted a career. He appreciated the four food groups, she was a die-hard sugar freak. Absolutely nothing, zero, *nada* in common.

And yet, when he recalled that glistening look of need in her eyes, the way her body had reacted to his, hell, the way her *mind* reacted to his, his gut told him, for all their external differences, internally they wanted the same thing.

Someone to love, maybe even a place to call home.

"I'm not having any dating days right now," Nigel muttered, sifting through the paint chips. He tossed that damn royal plum, not wanting to think again how well it would go with Kimberly's eyes. Tossed out a red-cherry color, too. Too much like her lips. He held up a greenish-yellow chip. "What do you think of Sunlit Ochre?"

"Man," Rigo said, staring at Nigel, "I knew you well enough in the ring to anticipate your next move, and know you well enough at this very moment to know you're throwing out what you like and settling for something else."

"We're talking about paint chips, right?"

Rigo rolled his eyes. "Sure, man."

"I'm open to other colors."

"Yeah?" Rigo took the Sunlit Ochre chip from Nigel and feigned matching it against the refrigerator, wall, then up against Nigel's face.

"It's not you," Rigo finally said. "Royal plum's better."

"Thought it was over the top."

Rigo nodded slowly, his dark eyes giving Nigel a knowing look. "It is." He paused, placed his hand on Nigel's shoulder. "Maybe, Nige, it's time to go after what you want."

5

LATER THAT SAME MORNING, the door to Life Dates opened and the drone of Vegas traffic merged with an old Bonnie Raitt tune playing on the radio. Maurice stopped harmonizing with Bonnie about love sneakin' up on you, strategically placed last month's *Spotlight* magazine with its feature article on Life Dates on the coffee table and looked up.

The door shut.

Bonnie crooned.

Maurice clutched his chest. "Cameron Diaz, step aside!"

Kimberly, her heels tap tapping across the parquet floor, smirked. "Honestly, Maurice. It's just a dress."

"Darling, darling," he cooed, doing a catwalk across the Oriental rug to her. He gestured up and down her outfit as though he were showing it off to an audience. "This is no dress. This—" he motioned for her to turn around, which, after a deep sigh, she reluctantly did "—this is a work of art."

"I just thought I'd wear a dress for a change," she murmured, avoiding his gaze.

After her shower this morning, Kimberly had started to pick out one of her suits to wear when she'd instead rifled through some dresses she kept in the back of her closet for special occasions—christenings, Easter brunch, her brother's wedding two-and-a-half years ago. She'd finally paused on a dress she'd never worn, which she vaguely recalled had been a hasty purchase for a birthday party she'd had to cancel attending at the last minute. The dress was yummy-soft to the touch, pretty in a forties film noir sort of way, and would go well with one of her work jackets.

She rarely did anything spontaneous, and for a moment she'd wondered if she was reacting to last night's experience with Nigel.

Maurice folded his hands and looked heavenward. "Finally, my prayers have been answered."

She frowned, walked over to the coffee table. Good. The *Spotlight* magazine was prominently displayed. "Honestly, Maurice, it's just a dress—"

"*Just* a *dress*?"

His woodsy cologne made an appearance before Maurice did. She glanced up, seeing he'd materialized in front of her, his tanned arms fisted on his designer-jean hips.

"This dress, my precious darling, combines the passionate primness of the forties with the slinkiness of the seventies. It's a fusion of Barbara Stanwyck and Bianca Jagger at their finest." He touched the padded shoulder of her jacket. "However, this has got to go."

"No."

"You look like a linebacker."

She sucked in a small breath. "Maurice, just as men wear jackets in business, I wear jackets. It commands respect."

Maurice crossed his arms over his tangerine polo shirt. "If I watched football, I'd say that jacket makes you look like so-and-so with his big, square shoulders, but suffice it to say you look like a generic linebacker."

Sometimes Maurice could get irritatingly focused on an issue. "First impressions—"

"Are everything. I know."

They stared at each other for a long, steely moment.

"It's too cold in here," she said tightly.

"Then I'll turn it down," he answered edgily, mostly to her jacket as though the two of them had a personal vendetta to work out.

And just as Kimberly was preparing her next sartorial verbal defense, dang if Maurice's eyes didn't go all soft on her. He had a way of turning those hard little brown eyes into soft puppy-dog ones. So sweet and tender, only some kind of black-hearted, soulless wench wouldn't forgive him for every nitpicky observation he'd ever made.

"Kimmy, I'm sorry about the linebacker comment," he murmured.

She sighed. "And I'm sorry for whatever I said in retaliation."

"You weren't bad this time. Just a variation of the same old, same old about how a woman must look like a man in the business world blah, blah, blah."

"But it's true!"

Maurice was feigning deafness, a habit she noticed he adopted whenever he wanted to switch the topic. Or get his way. He stepped forward and gingerly touched the dress fabric.

"Italian knit," he murmured appreciatively.

"I don't recall—"

"Darling, trust me. It is." He stepped back, tilted his head—the angle of his head showing off his diamond-stud earring—and looked her over. "Bias strips inserted into the seam line? Barbara Stanwyck is turning in her grave. And the color! That delicious rust just screams retro charm. Add your blond hair and coral lipstick—" he laid his manicured hand over his heart "—did I say Cameron Diaz?"

Kimberly nodded, totally recovered from the line-backer comment, more than a bit impressed he knew the fabric, and darn near eternally grateful for the Cameron Diaz reference.

"Forget Cameron," he suddenly said.

"I don't want to."

"No, you must, because I was wrong. Dressed like this, you could be Charlize Theron's twin. And *not* in that movie *Monster*."

She slid a glance at her reflection in the gold-veined mirror on the far wall. Charlize Theron? Really?

"Good. You're smiling. Okay, I'll accept you're addicted to wearing jackets," he said, heading to his desk, "but really, dear, someday you must do *something* with your hair." He flicked his wrist and checked the time. "Let me look at today's schedule. I think your next appointment is at—"

"Eleven. I know."

He shot her a look. "You peeked."

"No, I remembered."

"You never remember."

"I checked my home computer this morning and saw the entry in the Speedy Organizer file." It was an online calendar system Maurice had installed four months ago and which he loved to a fault. He updated it at least several times daily with appointments, notes, to-do lists. He even had her birthday—March 21, the first day of spring this year—highlighted with the notation "Kimmy's Birthday!"

"*You* checked the Speedy Organizer file?" He blinked dramatically. "You're right, it's too cold in here. I'll turn down the air-conditioning." He crossed the room to the thermostat.

Kimberly made a mental note to check Speedy Organizer more often. Not that she had an urge to become ultraorganized, but it was worth being one up on Maurice *occasionally*. Heading to her office, she paused at the crystal candy bowl on his desk. "What's this?"

"Yogurt-dipped soybeans."

"What happened to the jelly beans?"

"They have too much sugar, which makes you jittery. Soybeans are healthier. Especially for a woman of your age."

"Maurice! I'm only twenty-eight."

"Almost twenty-nine."

"That hardly qualifies as old."

"It's good to plan ahead, darling."

"Plan for what?"

"The change."

She shook her head. "I can't believe we're having this conversation. Menopause is light-years away. It's the hair. Or the jacket. You won't lighten up until I cut off one or burn the other."

"Oh, I do so hate playing the heavy," Maurice muttered dramatically as he walked back to his desk and sat down. He tapped a button on the keyboard. An online invoice displayed, and he started typing. "How was your coaching session last night with Yul Brynner?"

"Uh, okay," she said, suddenly absorbed with picking out a few soy-whatevers.

He gasped. "Oh, my God. You kissed him."

Kimberly looked up, adopting her best stoic look.

Maurice squinted, then gasped again. "Forget kissing. You did the whole enchilada!"

"None of your business." Oh, hell, who was she kidding? "Not quite the whole enchilada, but darn close. How'd you know?"

He pointed to his head. "Gay-dar. It never fails. And how you blushed when I asked about him." Maurice leaned his chin against his hand, giving her another of those puppy-dog looks. "You and Yul! This is better than *Beauty and the Beast!*"

"Maurice—"

He clapped his hands, cutting her off. "Okay, let's get a few things straight—no pun intended—right now." He grabbed a pad of paper and started taking notes. "Christina's is the best caterer in town, so we'll go with her."

"What's this 'we' business?"

"Michael & Angelo's is the *only* place for flowers. And before I forget, I'm your best man of honor because if you don't pick me I'll cause an outrageous scene at your wedding that you, your family and every one of your guests will never forget."

"I think I liked our menopause conversation better."

He shushed her with a wave of his hand. "Listen!" He pointed to the overhead speaker. "They're playing 'Unforgettable,' that Nat King Cole classic—"

Just then, the front door whooshed open.

Sunlight poured over a bronzed mountain of muscle and brawn stuffed into a body-clinging, turquoise T-shirt and khaki pants that molded thigh muscles.

"Good morning, Mr. Durand," said Maurice, with a look of surprise as though he hadn't just been planning the man's wedding and rest of his life. "Nice to see you again."

Kimberly eased in a slow breath, her pounding heart on the verge of drowning out ol' Nat.

"Good morning," Nigel said, his deep, rich voice rolling through the room.

He stepped inside and shut the door.

Last night had been unforgettable, unbearably unforgettable, the memories flickering over Kimberly like licking flames of heat. Although her hasty exit had been more unforgivable than unforgettable, but she'd had no choice.

Nigel took several steps toward her and stopped. "You look lovely, Ms. Logan."

Ms. Logan. Good. He's playing it aboveboard, professional. Exactly how they should be behaving. After all, last night was a mistake, a momentary lapse of judgment.

"Jersey knit," she rasped, followed by a high-pitched sound that sounded dangerously like a giggle. So much for professionalism.

"Italian," corrected Maurice, shooting her a get-it-together look.

"Right. Italian." *Yes, we're talking Italian knit here, all business, all jacket and bun, me boss, you client and I should never, ever have kissed you in the bar.*

"Mr. Durand," Maurice said, coming to the rescue, "may I offer you a cup of coffee or tea?"

Nigel's gaze remained locked with Kimberly's. "Actually, I just had… Yes, a cup of tea would be good."

Honest to God, Maurice was looking as pleased as if he'd arranged this little surprise meeting himself. Kimberly frowned. Had he? She wouldn't put anything above Maurice and his conniving, scheming, Speedy-Organizer ways.

"Peppermint? Ginseng? Rosebud?"

"Peppermint's fine."

"I'll get you a peppermint, too," Maurice said to Kimberly as he headed to the kitchenette.

"No, I'll have cof—"

Maurice shut the kitchenette door with a solid thud.

Kimberly turned back to face Nigel.

She gave a small roll of her shoulders.

Adjusted her jacket.

And started to say something, anything, but her senses were all tangled up, not helped one iota by the rich timbre of Nat King Cole's voice stroking the air, invoking steamy, hot memories of last night....

This is ridiculous. I'm a grown woman, the president of this business. I'm so above this juvenile meltdown just because I happened to... Something that had *never* happened before with a client, not *once* in the entire four years since she'd started this business.

Can't risk my professional reputation on this. Long ago she'd learned the power of hearsay, how a wrong action could ruin a girl's reputation, make it impossible to be respected in her community. Sure, this was Vegas, but if it was known Kimberly Logan had been intimate with one of her clientele, especially a professional wrestler known for his oiled body and leather Speedos, people would joke she'd switched from finding people *dates* to *escorts*.

I need to end his contract.

She raised her chin a notch. "Shall we sign the papers to terminate our contract now?"

The damn radio station segued into another sultry tune. Diana Krall was singing a moody version of "Steam Heat." Sssssss...steam heat... What was it with this station? Did they cater to nooners?

Nigel took in a deep breath, those pecs stretching that T-shirt to the max. "No. I don't want to terminate. I want us to go to the next step."

"The next step is for us to be sensible, find you another agency, and—"

"I believe the next step is 'How to make a woman melt.'"

Toe-curling memories of last night's lovemaking came rushing back, and for a sizzling moment, she and Nigel shared a look that said he'd succeeded exceptionally well at that step.

As though on cue, Maurice sashayed back into the room with two cups of steaming tea, one in a delicate pink cup, the other in a bold-patterned mug. Scents of peppermint traced the air. He hummed along with Diana Krall, then stopped and said "oh" so innocently,. "You two want to sit here or in Ms. Logan's office?"

"Here."

"Ms. Logan's office," Nigel said at the same time.

"Ms. Logan's office it is," Maurice said, carrying the cups into the far room.

Moments later, Kimberly sat behind her desk, a replay of two days ago when Nigel sat in the chair opposite her. Only, it felt as if a lot more than forty-eight hours had passed. The rooster logo had evolved into a bad-boy T. His distrustful look had softened to one of tenderness.

She glanced down at her dress, took a mental pulse of her emotions and realized no man had ever affected her like this, so quickly and powerfully, and she hated it. She was *way* out of her comfort zone. How many times had she counseled clients to monitor their expectations, to pace themselves and not expect overnight results.

To not believe in love at first sight.

The last thought stunned her more than anything else she'd been thinking. Love at first sight? Is *that* what had happened between her and Nigel?

No.

No way.

That was not only unreal, it was surreal.

She lifted her cup and took a sip, buying time.

Nigel did the same.

After what seemed a small forever of their sipping and listening to Maurice harmonize with Diana Krall in the other room, Nigel broke the silence.

"I can't stay long."

"Oh?"

"I, uh, have a date."

"A date?"

"Well, not a *date* exactly, but an appointment."

An *appointment*, well, that was different. Not that she cared.

"For lunch." Nigel glanced at the clock on her wall. "It's almost eleven-ten. I need to be at Doolittle Park by eleven-thirty." Nigel shifted in his chair. "Care to, uh, join us?"

"Us?"

"Me and Austin. He's a kid I've been working with this past year, part of the Mentor-Mentee Program."

I'm not dating Nigel. Shouldn't be dating him. I've let things go too far, need to reel it in, take charge.

"I'm sorry, I can't," she said in her best professional voice. "I also have an appointment, actually it was for eleven, which means he or she is running late—"

"It's been canceled," Maurice called out in a sing-song from the other room.

After an awkward moment, Nigel grinned. "Looks like you're free, Ms. Logan."

She wanted to stay in the role of Ms. President, but instead Kimberly got caught up in the infectiousness of Nigel's smile, the way his eyes sparkled, and damn if she didn't find herself returning his smile.

"What'd you have for breakfast?" Nigel asked.

She flicked a glance at her partially closed door, knowing you-know-who was on the other side, straining to hear every single word. If she lied, he'd singsong the corrected version.

"Some yogurt-soy things," she admitted.

Nigel shook his head. "Can't run a car on no gasoline," he said, standing. "There's a sandwich place near the park. Like turkey?"

She nodded.

"Coleslaw?"

"Sure."

"Great. You, Austin and I will have a picnic." He set his mug on a side table. "You might get too hot with that jacket on."

"I'll be fine," she said, standing, ignoring Maurice's audible gasp from the other room. But she'd broil in this jacket before taking it off. It symbolized her professional status, which was more critical than ever to hold on to.

Besides, deep down, she feared if she took it off, the rest of her inhibitions would come tumbling off again, too.

6

Step three: Make women melt, part I

ALMOST TWENTY MINUTES LATER, Nigel drove his Jeep down Mead Boulevard, scanning Doolittle Park. No Austin. Nigel checked the clock on his dashboard. Eleven-thirty. Not that he'd expected Austin to arrive early, or even on time, but Nigel always held out hope.

He pulled over and parked.

After getting out, he headed around the front of the vehicle and opened Kimberly's door. A dry breeze whipped through the front seat, lifting the hem of her dress. Nigel caught a flash of thigh before Kimberly's manicured hand pressed the dress back down.

He hadn't thought of her as demure before, but after that fast save he wondered. But when he recalled last night, he knew this hothouse orchid could let down her guard and be deliciously *un*demure.

He helped her down. She teetered a little as she got her footing on the ground.

"You can take those off," he said, gesturing to her heels. "It'll be easier for you to walk barefoot. The park is mostly sand and this time of year it's warm, not hot."

"Wouldn't matter if it was nicely chilled, the answer is no."

The determined look on Kimberly's face told him she wasn't parting with her shoes. He wouldn't *even* mention her leaving the jacket in the car after her speech earlier.

"Your choice." They still held hands. It amazed Nigel how small and soft hers was, how white against his brown skin.

She almost looked shy as she slipped her hand from his.

"Let's go to that picnic table," he said, pointing to the nearest wooden table under a palm tree. At least she wouldn't have to walk far and it'd be easy for Austin to see them there.

After they sat down, Nigel laid out the food and drinks. A twittering bird soared through the hazy sky. He scanned the area, appreciating the sweet-scented piñon pines and flowering yuccas. Several toddlers, under the watchful eyes of their mothers, squealed and laughed in a nearby playground.

"Our days of being outdoors are numbered," he said wistfully, setting one of the cola cans on the napkins so they wouldn't blow away. In a few months, the daytime temperatures would soar to the hundreds, making Vegas one big shimmering heat wave.

"I never go outside unless it's on my way to more air-conditioning," said Kimberly, adjusting her dress as she sat down on the bench opposite him. "Now, about your contract—"

"You never go outside, take day trips?" he asked, cutting her off. "Even during winter? Some of the most gorgeous scenery in the world is just outside the city."

She paused. "You're not going to let me discuss business, are you?"

"That's right. We're having a picnic. Think of it as a mini day trip."

"Speaking, then, of day trips…" Kimberly waggled her fingers in the general direction of outside the city. "Seen one desert, you've seen them all."

"I beg to differ. The red rock formations in the Valley of Fire are awe inspiring."

She gave him a funny look. "Do I look like a rock-formation kind of girl?"

Nigel opted to not respond. He didn't know what a rock-formation girl looked like, but he did know Kimberly Logan needed to learn a thing or two about the land she lived in. Vegas was a hell of a lot more than the neon-studded Strip with its casinos and flashy shows.

Tucking that thought away, he started unwrapping his sandwich.

"Aren't we going to wait for Austin?"

"He knows what time we're meeting, and he's late." Nigel took a bite of his sandwich.

Kimberly started to say something, then changed her mind. She began unwrapping her sandwich.

After they had eaten in silence for several minutes,

a kid on a dirt bike rode up to the table, the tails of his unbuttoned Hawaiian shirt flapping behind him. The sun glinted off a gold earring and a heavy chain around his neck. He spun to a stop, the wheels kicking up sand.

Kimberly stared at him, her eyes bigger than Nigel had ever seen. He felt like warning her she hadn't seen *anything* yet.

"Hello, Austin," Nigel said.

The kid dropped his bike on the ground while staring at Kimberly, whose gaze dipped to take in the red-white-and-blue dice tattoo over his heart.

She swallowed, set down her sandwich. "Hi."

Silence.

"I'm Kimberly."

"Austin." He cocked a look at Nigel.

"She's my friend."

Austin snorted, plopped down at the far end of the bench. He pulled the band off his ponytail, shaking loose his dark, shoulder-length hair.

Nigel pushed a sandwich down the table, acting as though the chip on the kid's shoulder wasn't the size of a tree stump. Life hadn't been easy for the fifteen-year-old boy. An absentee father, a drug-addicted mother, two younger sisters from another man who dropped in and out of his mother's life.

By age thirteen, Austin had developed a skill for breaking into homes and stealing electronic equipment that he'd pawn. And, something Nigel had yet to figure out, Austin had liked to steal paintings, too, but those he didn't pawn. Which might have made sense if the pieces were collectibles. But no, the kid had a thing for kitschy paintings. Like the amateurish blue-and-pink cactus by a middle-aged car salesman, a Mr. Wahlberg, who to this day was dumbstruck that some punk kid stole *that* instead of his microwave.

After Austin's third offense, a judge gave him a choice—do time in juvy or enter a state-sponsored program called the Mentor-Mentee Program. The program matched troubled kids with responsible adults who helped the child stay on track with school, goals, career. Austin, not wanting to lose his freedom, grudgingly chose the program.

Nigel had tried to pick spots and events that might spark an interest in the sullen, moody boy. Most kids would have given their eyeteeth to meet some of Nigel's pro-wrestling buddies—the Mortician, Rigo the Wrecker—but Austin acted bored. Nigel, undeterred, had tried other ideas. A NASCAR race, even special backstage passes for an Aerosmith concert. Damn if the kid didn't behave like it was just one big game, which Nigel knew was an act. But he was clueless as to how to break through to the boy.

"I'm thinking of getting a new tattoo," Austin suddenly said, ignoring the sandwich in front of him.

"No, you're not," Nigel said.

A car rambled down Mead Boulevard, its muffler coughing.

"What kind of tattoo?" Kimberly asked.

Nigel gave her a look, which she ignored.

"A tarantula," Austin said, mimicking spider legs with his stretched-out fingers.

She didn't flinch. "Funny, I'd thought you pick something more colorful."

A look of surprise flickered across the boy's face. He shrugged, obviously more intrigued with her response than he dared let on.

"Because of your tattoo," she continued, waggling a finger at the red-white-and-blue dice. "And your, uh…" She pointed at her nose, a reference to the tiny silver-and-ruby stud in his.

Austin looked away, flicked his tongue along his bottom lip, then turned back and met Kimberly's gaze. "I'd been thinking of a pirate."

She raised her eyebrows. "Like Johnny Depp in *Pirates of the Caribbean?*"

Austin shrugged.

"That makes sense," she said with a kick-back chatty style Nigel had never seen with her. "Colorful, bigger than life, adventurous." She picked a tomato off her sandwich. "Just like you, I bet."

Austin shrugged again, shyly looking at Kimberly. After a pause, he asked, "What do you do?"

"I run a dating agency."

Austin slid a look at Nigel.

"I signed up with her agency," he explained. It was his personal goal to always be honest with Austin, hoping that if he himself modeled the behavior, the kid might want to adopt that trait himself.

"Meet anybody?" Austin asked.

Nigel bit his inner cheek, cursing himself for his vow of honesty. If he said no, he'd be lying. And Austin—who never missed a thing—would know.

"Yes," Nigel muttered.

A rose hue crept up Kimberly's neck.

Which Austin observed with a wry smile. "Cool," he finally said, reaching for his sandwich.

The rest of lunch was the most pleasant Nigel had ever experienced with the boy. Austin talked about everything from his bike to how much he hated his gym teacher who insisted Austin try out for the high school soccer team.

"You should try out," Nigel said.

"No way."

"I never understood soccer," chimed in Kimberly. "I mean, the guys are cute as all get out—" she did a little shimmy movement that Nigel would ponder for days "—but all those balls bouncing off people's heads." With a roll of her eyes, she took a sip of her drink, swallowed. "I just don't get it."

Austin snorted. "Yeah. It sucks."

"Is there a Beckham somebody who's a soccer star?" she asked.

"David Beckham," answered Austin.

"Right. He's married to that rock star."

"Posh," said Austin.

"Right. Posh. You know, it's amazing how many women have come into my agency saying they want a man who looks like David Beckham." Kimberly smiled sweetly from Austin to Nigel. "He's okay looking," she said conspiratorially, "but I think it's really all those lean, toned muscles from running around that soccer field that make women nuts."

She said women wanted a man just like The Phantom. Nigel wasn't sure whether to feel jealous that women apparently drooled, too, over this Beckham fellow or be impressed at Kimberly's savvy business schmoozing. Considering Austin was not looking sullen, but interested, Nigel opted for a mix of both. He'd never found the key to what interested Austin, but Kimberly appeared to have struck a chord in the kid within minutes of meeting him.

Nigel was more than a little impressed with her people skills. No wonder she was such a successful businesswoman.

A few minutes later, Austin tossed his empty wrapper into a nearby trash can. "Gotta go," he mumbled, standing.

"Next week, same day? Time?" asked Nigel.

"Can't make it at eleven-thirty." Austin picked up his bike.

"Twelve-thirty?" asked Nigel.

"Sure."

"Nice meeting you, Austin," Kimberly said.

Nigel was surprised at the sweetness that suddenly crowded the boy's face.

"Nice to meet you, too." He mounted his bike. But rather than peel out as he usually did, he just sat and tapped his sandaled foot against the pedal.

"You coming again next week, too?" he suddenly asked.

Kimberly paused, looked at Nigel. He nodded.

"I'd love to," she said.

"Cool." Austin looked at Nigel. "See you next week."

As he rode off, Nigel fought a well of emotion. He'd grown up the older brother who told his sisters when and how to abide by family rules and later insisted their dates do the same. He'd done what he'd seen his father do—enforce family policies. Lovingly enforce them, but with strength. Dad's word was, after all, the law.

This entire past year, he'd blamed Austin for not stepping up to the plate when, he now belatedly realized, it had been him who hadn't. He'd done as he had done growing up—imposed his world onto the boy's rather than invite himself into Austin's world.

Which Kimberly had done.

She'd never once overreacted to Austin's in-your-face attitude. No, she'd been quietly resilient—surprising, considering her control-freak tendencies. She'd observed how Austin loved color by referencing his tattoo. Validated the boy's good qualities by comparing them to an adventurous pirate's. And the coup of the year—she'd slyly encouraged Austin to give soccer a try with that "women love those lean, toned muscles" comment.

Very smooth.

Very insightful.

"Kimberly," Nigel said, then paused. There were so many things he wanted to say. But just as he'd had trouble reading Austin, it wasn't exactly a piece of cake to figure out what made Kimberly tick. Or what might tick her off. So instead he touched her hand. "You're okay."

They held each other's gaze for a long moment.

"You, too," she whispered.

"I want to continue our relationship."

She said nothing, her gray eyes observing him.

"Our business relationship, of course," he said, withdrawing his hand and gathering their trash off the table. This was why he blew it at dating—he had a knack for saying or doing something over-the-top dumb-ass at inopportune moments. "I'd like you to continue coaching me." He sucked in a fortifying breath. "Here's the deal. I realize you're not ready for…more, so I won't pursue that. Instead, I'll back off and you can take me to the next step."

Was that a look of disappointment he saw in her eyes? Or his wishful male ego imagining things.

"It's not appropriate for me to—"

"Cross the line. I know."

She nodded.

"I don't want you to compromise your professional standards. I mean that. But selfishly, I don't want to go elsewhere and start over. Besides, isn't the customer always right?"

"No."

"Humor me."

A smile curved her mouth, and he thought how pretty she looked when she smiled. How he wished he could make her smile like that more often.

Yes, he'd meant it when he said he didn't want her to compromise her professional standards, but if she'd give him a chance, she'd discover this wasn't about compromise but about two people who'd stumbled onto something potentially good.

"I'll humor you," he said, "if you'll humor me."

She blinked, smoothed a hand down her jacket. "No more…"

"No." *Not unless you ask.*

"I think we can wrap up your steps within a few weeks."

"But I thought it would take three months." He was more of a threat than he'd realized.

"Tops." She fanned a hand on her flushed face. "With you, I'm fairly certain we can wrap this up quickly."

"Okay." He paused. "What step am I on?"

She stood, eased herself over the bench. "You got the bad-boy look and act down, so we'll resume with making women melt." She avoided his eyes as she swiped along her hairline.

"Okay."

"I'll meet you on the bridge at Bellagio's next Monday night, nine o'clock."

"Monday?" He frowned. "That's almost a week away."

She nodded. "I have other clients, you know. Plus, Bellagio will be less crowded on a Monday."

True, it was one of the most popular sites in Sin City. Designed after Italy's Lake Como, the Bellagio was famous for its spectacular dancing fountains and botanical gardens, which were draws for the locals, as well, considering this oasis of water and foliage sat smack in the middle of a vast desert.

"All right. I'll meet you on the Bellagio bridge. Although I'm clueless how I'm supposed to make women melt there."

"Oh, that's just the beginning," Kimberly said, walking back to his Jeep, the hem of her dress fluttering provocatively on a passing breeze.

Step three: Make women melt, part II

SIX DAYS, eight hours and fifteen minutes later, Kimberly Logan was sweating. Not perspiring.

Sweating.

She'd call it a full-tilt anxiety attack, but she'd never had one in her life. Hell, she'd given talks to rooms filled with several hundred people and she'd never sweated one nervous flop-sweat drop.

No, she was sweating because she was melting.

Melting at the thought of seeing Nigel again.

Worse, she'd arrived *early.* A first for Kimberly Logan.

She paced a few feet on the bridge leading into the Bellagio, eyeing the man-made lake and its numerous fountains that surged, sparkled and exploded in time to an old Frank Sinatra tune that blasted over the audio system. He was crooning how his woman looked tonight and how it touched his foolish heart.

Kimberly tugged on her yellow, short-sleeve jacket that matched her A-line yellow cotton dress. Simple. She'd kept it simple. Another first for Kimberly. But earlier, after nearly succumbing to a minibreakdown trying to figure out what to wear—*determined* not to look regimented or, God forbid, like a linebacker— keeping it simple was a relief.

Or she told herself it was about keeping it simple. A niggling voice kept whispering she wanted to look appealing to Nigel.

She checked her watch for the nth time. 8:58. This was ridiculous, pacing and checking her watch. *Maybe I should get a drink, or go to visit the ladies' room, or…*

And then she saw him.

Nigel walked through the crowd, which parted for the mammoth-size man, people's heads turning upward with looks of awe and surprise. A few people appeared to recognize him, nudging each other and whispering. Some of the attention turned her way as people caught the way he looked at her, realizing she obviously was the reason he was here.

They're probably wondering if I'm his date, maybe even his wife. And for a silly, giddy moment, Kimberly succumbed to the fantasy, wondering how it'd feel for the two of them to be an item.

He stopped, signed an autograph. He was nice

to total strangers, which made Kimberly feel momentarily guilty for flipping off that driver who'd cut her off in traffic earlier. Nigel laughed, tousled a boy's hair, and continued walking toward her.

Tonight he wore a pair of dress pants with a flesh-colored T-shirt underneath a vanilla-colored linen jacket.

Nice.

She'd told him to dress "bad boy" but at this moment, who cared? The man oozed class and confidence, topped by that smooth bald dome that screamed "touch me."

Stealthily wiping her moistened fingertips against her dress, she made a mental note to rethink her bad-boy dress code in the future.

He finally reached her and stopped.

She slowly tilted back her head as her gaze crawled up his body.

The linen jacket was unbuttoned, the stretched T-shirt revealing his flat waist and the sharp-edged detail of his chest. The shoulders of the jacket didn't disguise the heavy swell of muscles along his shoulders and upper arms. And, above it all, a tanned face that gleamed like bronze against the cream of his jacket. Funny, she hadn't noticed before how thick and long his lashes were. Although that night when he'd made love to her, she'd certainly noticed how, underneath those dark eyebrows, those killer baby blues were the hottest, sexiest she'd ever seen.

Her muscles tightened and a feeling like warm honey poured through her body.

Sinatra's sultry voice hit a soulful crescendo. The fountains soared, the water infused with vibrant red and orange lights. Nigel's familiar scent—masculine, that touch of citrusy cologne—swirled around her.

I'm going to die of sensory overload, right here on the bridge to Bellagio.

"You okay?" asked Nigel, cupping her elbow with his hand. "You look a little pale."

"I'm fine," she lied.

"Have you eaten today?"

"Maurice made me eat a vegan burger." She still wasn't sure what vegan was, but it had made Maurice happy so she'd complied. The past few days she'd decided life would be easier if she occasionally *flowed* with some of Maurice's wishes instead of fighting them. "And a side of fries."

"Vegan burger and a side of fries?" Nigel laughed, the sound rich and deep. He gave her an admiring look. "Told you cars run better with gasoline."

"Yes, you did," she whispered, basking in his approval. She hadn't felt like this in years. Like a kid. Thrilled to have done or said something pleasing.

"I watched that movie *9 1/2 Weeks*," he said, lowering his voice, "just like you asked."

"G-good." And just when she thought she'd overcome sensory overload, images of the erotic-food-foreplay kitchen scene from the film seared through her brain. Followed rapidly by a memory of Nigel commenting that he was remodeling his kitchen.

She wondered if that film had inspired him on ways to christen the new room.

"And I read *101 Ways to Make Her Melt*."

"Yess," she whispered, certain her libido had surged several hundred feet along with the hyperactive fountains. *101 Ways* was the guide she asked men to read so they could brush up on—she *never* said learn—flirting techniques. Kimberly had rattled off those two homework assignments to Nigel on the drive back to her office after the picnic last Tuesday, giving him the instructions in her best professional voice, never dreaming how they'd come back to bite her.

Bite.

She suppressed a shiver, remembering the delicious sensation of his lips and teeth nibbling her.

I'm losing it. I was the one who insisted on the coach-client relationship. I was the one who said we'd help him make other *women melt.*

Oh, how the mighty fall.

"Let's go inside," she muttered, easing her arm from Nigel's protective grip. She reminded herself how tough it'd been to rebuild her life. How it had taken all of her resources—emotional and financial—to relocate to Las Vegas, a sprawling metropolis where nobody knew her the way they had back home. Or cared about her past. Reminded herself of the excruciatingly long, hard hours she'd put into building her business.

Reminded herself that Nigel Durand was well-known in certain Vegas circles. All he needed was to tell the wrong person about how he'd signed up with Life Dates and gotten involved with its president to ruin her reputation, personally and professionally.

Even if they weren't in this owner-client relationship, it would never work. He wanted the white picket fence. She wanted the high-rise. He loved his family. She was estranged from hers. And on and on....

There was the right woman for him, and it wasn't Kimberly.

She turned, motioning for Nigel to accompany her toward the Bellagio lobby, to the place where she'd coach him on making *other* women melt.

As they walked away, Frank's song ended, the water fading into clouds of mist.

7

Step three: Make women melt, part III

A FEW MINUTES LATER, Nigel followed Kimberly through the Bellagio lobby and its expanse of white marble and gold trim broken up by splashes of red, yellow and orange from extravagant floral displays. Birds twittered. Butterflies fluttered. And above it all hung an expansive glass chandelier, its translucent, color-streaked globes spreading mushroomlike along the ceiling.

He'd been in this lobby before, and every time thought the same thing. That only in Las Vegas did artificial nature dare to compete with the real thing.

Kimberly suddenly stopped and turned. She gestured toward an after-hours bar off the lobby from which the buzz of conversations and tinkling of glass could be heard.

She tucked a wisp of blond hair back into her chignon. "Don't walk too fast when you go in."

"What?"

She waggled her pink-manicured nails in the general direction of his feet. "Pigeon-toed."

He wanted to mention he was two-hundred-and-eighty pounds of rock-hard, chiseled muscle and did she *really* think the opposite sex dropped their baby blues to check out his size fourteens when he walked into a room?

"Right," he growled. "Slow."

"And remember, keep your lines simple and real. No tried-and-true clichés."

He glanced at her hair, remembering the night he'd told her it was the color of sunshine. He thought back to the story of *Rapunzel*, which had been his youngest sister's favorite fairy tale. Rapunzel had long golden hair that fell in a shimmering carpet of curls for her beloved prince to climb.

"I'll keep it simple," he murmured, wondering how far Kimberly's hair would fall if she'd let it tumble loose. The night he'd made love to her, she'd left before he got to see.

"And remember, let women touch you first."

"My hands are tied."

Kimberly paused, a confused look pinching her delicate features.

"Women must touch me first," he explained, "because, hypothetically, my hands are tied." He held up his tan, fisted hands and crossed them at the wrists.

She stared for a long, drawn-out moment. "Yes," she said, her voice catching. "I see."

He wondered if she had any idea how she looked right now. Her eyes large and dewy, her cheeks a tell-

tale pink against that almost prim butter-yellow outfit. Like a hot and bothered all-grown-up Pollyanna.

She fumbled with the top button of her jacket, finally undoing the top two, which exposed the
flushed skin of her chest and neck.

"One more thing." She touched him lightly on his
jacket.

Let the woman touch you first.

"After watching *9 1/2 Weeks*," she continued, "and
reading *101 Ways to Make Her Melt*, you should have
a good sense of sensual mannerisms, suggestive
phrases, verbal innuendoes..." She made a rolling
motion of her hand that he took to mean "and so on
and so forth."

But that look in her eye said she was recalling that
night when he did all of that and more.

"Right," he whispered huskily.

"Right..." she echoed, then paused. He couldn't
tell if she'd run out of breath or was stopping and
waiting for his reaction. This sure as hell wasn't the
Kimberly he'd met a week ago. Easily flustered,
dressing softer, showing up on time more often than
not. Despite her "we're professionals" stance, he'd
gotten to her.

And if he played *his* game right, the good guy underneath some bad-boy facade, maybe she'd let
down her guard again. Maybe, eventually, she'd
even open her heart to him.

*Take it slow. Keep your lines simple. Think about your
sensual mannerisms.*

He put his hand on hers, which still touched his jacket, and let the heat of her skin mingle with his. Such soft, silky skin.

"Trust me," he said, giving her hand a squeeze. "I'll make good use of my sensual mannerisms, suggestive phrases, verbal innuendoes."

She laughed, a bit too nervously. "Well, that should actually be saved for—"

"The next step," he finished for her, letting his fingers interlace with hers. "Kiss her 'til she…" His gaze dropped to her curvaceous, pink-frosted lips, remembering how it had felt to kiss her.

"Whimpers," Kimberly concluded.

He paused, rubbing his thumb ever so slowly along the outside of hers. "Excuse me?"

She parted her lips, eased in a shaky breath. "*Wh-whimpers.*"

"Hmm?" He tightened his hold on her hand.

"Whim—" She stopped short. "Either you have a hearing problem or you're making me repeat the word whimpers."

"Would I do that?" He slid his thumb into the cushion of her palm and kneaded the soft, hidden flesh.

She uttered a small gasp, and he swore he could feel her shudder all the way down to her fingertips.

And for a long moment they just stood there, the hubbub of people checking in, the trill of birds receding into the background. It was just him and Kimberly, the small fires he saw deep in her eyes, the querulous smile on her needing-to-be-kissed lips, and had he ever noticed before the tiny dimple in her chin? He couldn't wait for the day, the hour, the very moment she asked him to kiss her again. Because that's how it would be—she'd ask. She'd make the first move, and he'd gladly make the second, third…

She blinked, as though slowly awakening. "I think we've covered everything."

He nodded, thinking how wrong she was.

Easing her hand from his, she said, "As your success coach, I'll be nearby."

He didn't think she sounded too sure of her role. He liked that.

"Not too close, just close enough to observe you, take notes."

Wait a minute. "You'll be taking notes?"

"Certainly." She pulled out a small, leather-bound notepad and held it up.

"Look, I'm willing to work through whatever step we're on, but I'm not wild about my every move being graded. I don't want to look up and see you holding up a piece of paper with the number four scrawled on it."

That dimpled, determined chin notched up. "This isn't the Olympics. I'm not judging you. This is part of the—"

"Just agree with me on this one, okay?"

She stammered something unintelligible, obviously taken aback at his no-way attitude. Then, after several rapid blinks, she found her voice. "I'll not take copious notes."

Which he knew was as good as he was going to get. "Okay, let's get this show on the road."

"One more thing."

He cocked an eyebrow.

"If you and I should happen to speak inside, I'm calling you Nicky."

He'd almost forgotten about the name thing. "Why? So any women within earshot will think that's my bad-boy name?"

"It's for me." She smoothed her hand over her jacket. "I need to call you Nicky. To help me distance myself from you."

"Sure," he said, wondering if she had any idea that her clothes, her body language, said loud and clear she was growing closer to him, not further.

"Sure," he repeated, savoring the thrill of winning, "call me Nicky."

And with a cocksure, bad-boy wink, he sauntered off—slowly—toward the bar.

KIMBERLY PURPOSEFULLY waited in the lobby a few minutes before following him.

She needed a moment to gather her wits, have some space.

Space to breath, relax, try not to obsess on how Nigel's—Nicky, dammit, Nicky's—hand had felt wrapped around hers. *His hands are so big.* Or how deliciously sensual his touch could be. *Hard to believe he used to throttle wrestlers with those hands.*

Or how exquisitely good the mere pressing of a

thumb against her palm could feel. Feeling her bare skin against his made her wish their one night of passion had been more, well, mutual. She wished she'd seen all of him, felt the length of his body against hers. Wished she'd tasted him, given him as much pleasure as he'd given her....

She glanced at an ornately carved, gilded mirror on the wall. Her face was flushed, as though hot with fever.

Calm down, girl.

She rummaged in her purse, found a tin of mints—Outrageously Minty—and popped one into her mouth. As a blast of spearmint shot straight to her brain, she rolled back her shoulders and headed toward the bar.

Whereas the lobby was light-filled with white marble everywhere, the bar was submerged in shadows and moody lighting. She'd always liked bringing her clients to this place. Its darkened atmosphere provided a sense of anonymity where nervous clients could more comfortably practice their wooing techniques. Plus, it was mostly frequented by out-of-towners, so a local needn't be overly concerned they'd run into people they knew.

Kimberly sidled through the crowd, cursing under her breath as she stumbled not once, but *twice*, as she maneuvered around groups of people. *Darn these new shoes.* A pair of Prada mules that had seemed fine when she'd walked into the Bellagio earlier, but didn't want to behave when she had to do sudden turns, it appeared. She'd bought the shoes on a whim because the color matched her new yellow dress.

That was the problem with whims. If you weren't careful, they could get you into trouble.

That's why, after a client started connecting with prospective mates, Kimberly took the time to discuss the importance of shared values and goals, common interests, often adding nuggets of wisdom from her motivational tapes.

She made a mental note to do that with Nig— Nicky. She didn't want him falling hard for the first woman who made goo-goo eyes at him without knowing what made her tick. And Kimberly also needed to remind him to cool it with the brownie baking and sitting next to the phone until after step six. He'd been too available before and he needed to learn the value of mystery. After all, it wasn't just men who enjoyed the chase. Nig—Nicky, needed to allow himself to be pursued.

A minute later, she slid onto a stool and set her purse on the polished wood surface. She caught a man's gaze in the mirror behind the neatly lined-up bottles. He grinned lasciviously, his teeth lost underneath a rangy salt-and-pepper moustache. He wriggled his eyebrows and winked.

She cut him a you've-got-to-be-kidding look before breaking eye contact to look around for…Nicky.

Who was easy to spot. That bulked-up silhouette nearly blocked out the wall aquarium he stood in front of.

She pulled out the remnant of a granola bar—courtesy of Maurice—that she'd been nibbling in the car on the ride over here. Her eyes were adjusting to the light, so she could better see the forms huddled around Nicky.

A tall woman stood to his left, dressed in white slacks that showed off her slim figure and a T-shirt that revealed she wasn't wearing a bra. Really, in this darkened room if Kimberly could see a woman was braless, that meant up close, Nicky probably saw…

With a snort, she whipped out her notepad and jotted down a note before looking up again. The braless wonder was tossing back her overcoiffed mane and laughing.

Nicky, *funny?*

Kimberly frowned, trying to recall if he'd ever told *her* a joke. Surely he hadn't because she'd remember laughing, right? Of course, Maurice accused her of not laughing much—okay, at all—but then Maurice wasn't exactly Jay Leno.

Kimberly jotted down another note.

And looked up.

A petite number in a peach-colored clingy dress had joined the see-through-T-shirt woman, who probably laughed at anything, and Nicky. *Two women?* Kimberly glanced at her watch. He'd only been here—what?—ten minutes?

And he already had *two* women?

"What'll you have?"

She looked at the bartender, a slightly balding man

with the unruffled demeanor of someone who'd been working Vegas for a long time.

"I'll have a diet cola, with a slice of—"

A peal of laughter diverted her attention.

Kimberly slid a look over her shoulder.

What? A *third* woman had joined Nicky's entourage?

Some redhead in a leather halter top that rode *way* too high and exposed her tummy. And those pants— hadn't Red heard spandex was passé a decade ago?

Kimberly bit off another bite of her granola bar and chewed, hard, suddenly hating this boring yellow ensemble she was wearing. *The skirt reaches my knees, for God's sake.* Worse, this morning she'd slipped on her one-hundred-percent-cotton bra with matching underwear. Both a mottled purple from her accidentally tossing her grape-colored pullover in with the whites that month her housekeeper was sick and Kimberly was forced to bungle her way through the laundry.

Skirts that hit her knees. Cotton, tie-dyed underclothes. Wow, was she hot or what?

"Diet cola with a slice of?" prompted the bartender, sliding a napkin toward her.

She always ordered cola, always wore her hair in a chignon, always drove the same way to work so she didn't get stuck in traffic.

She couldn't think of the last time she'd done something different.

Fun.

Wild.

Well, except for that night with Nigel… That hot, wonderful night….

"I want a pink drink," she blurted.

The bartender didn't miss a beat, which made her realize he'd probably heard every line in the book.

"Pink Cadillac? Tequila Sunrise? Cosmopolitan?"

"What did they drink on *Sex in the City*?"

He nodded to another customer who was flagging him down. "Cosmopolitan."

"I'll have one of those," Kimberly said, glancing at Nicky and his trio of Laughing, Sluttily Dressed Nubiles. "Make it a double."

"AND THEN THERE WAS THE TIME I hammered The Mortician thirty-eight seconds into the first round," recounted Nigel, making eye contact with each of the women—Gigi, Patty and—did the petite one in that body-hugging dress say her name was Cara or Carol?

They all stared back, hanging on his every word.

Hanging on parts of his body, too, from the feel of hands on his biceps, his waist and a few seconds ago he was fairly certain someone had copped a feel of his butt.

The redhead twittered, did a little shoulder wriggle that made her breasts jiggle underneath that leather-bondage top. "Thirty-eight seconds," she repeated in a breathless whisper as though she'd never heard of such an astounding feat in her life.

"But that's only in the ring, right?" said Cara-

Carol. She made a little growling sound. "I bet you last a lot longer elsewhere…."

There was a time when this would have been entertaining. Enticing, even. But he'd had his share of women who wanted him for what he appeared to be, not who he was, and not being wanted for who you really are gets old, fast. He had no doubt if he asked any of them if they liked gooey homemade brownies or a play-day where they'd picnic and fly kites, their teasing come-on looks would glaze over into ones of utter boredom.

He looked over at the bar where he'd seen Kimberly sit down, the spot currently blocked by a couple of guys swigging beers. Seemed a bit hokey to take notes, but if it meant the opportunity to be alone with her again to review them, well, baby, that's why he was here. To play the game.

The guys moved, and Nigel caught sight of Kimberly sitting at the bar.

Overhead lights spilled in golden drops onto the highly polished bar, the gold emphasizing her yellow outfit and blond hair. She looked almost fairy tale-like, wrapped in a gauzy golden cloud.

Except for that drink.

Nigel squinted. She was polishing off some big pink drink. One of those lethal, liquid candy kinds that went down real easy and hit real hard.

Wait, was the bartender sliding *another* of those pink bombs toward her?

How many had she already had?

Gigi, who seemed to be showing even more of her tummy than when she'd first joined the group, squeezed his bicep and whispered, "So tell us about the time you choke-slammed Rigo the Wrecker after he attempted a Stunner."

"He didn't feel so good," Nigel muttered, glowering at Kimberly as she started to suck down the new drink.

"Gotta go," he said, extricating himself.

He cut a path to the bar, pushing several guys out of the way when they didn't make room. One started to bark something about who the hell did he think he was, but shut up when Nigel shot him a look.

"I'll take that," he said, sliding onto the stool next to her. He took the pink concoction from her hand.

Kimberly did an exaggerated double take. "'Scuse me?"

"You've had enough." He set the glass out of her reach.

She waggled a manicured nail at the glass. "That's a Cosmopolitan!"

"Good for it. I'm taking you home."

Kimberly flashed him a defiant look. Which, if she hadn't been sitting at an angle, might have been imposing. "Nobody orders me around."

"Shame. Might do you good sometimes." He picked up her notepad, saw a few scrawled notes about women who should wear bras and women who laughed too much. He frowned, slipped it in her purse. "Is there anything else you need?"

"The rest of my drink."

"Focused on a goal, as always," he murmured, helping her off the stool. She fell slightly against him, her hair soft against his cheek. It smelled fresh and clean, with a hint of apricots.

"Look, I'll buy you a nice, chilled water at the gift shop on the way out. You'll feel better in the morning for it, trust me."

She looked up at him, batting her long lashes. "I'd love to feel better in the morning," she said with a slow, secret smile.

Great. One oversize Cosmopolitan, and Kimberly Logan was ready to play femme fatale. Although his baser side longed to play tease-me-take-me, he never took advantage of a woman who'd been drinking. *Never.* That little rule had been drummed into him by his sweet-tempered Grandmother Alice who told him, at the age of fifteen, that if he ever took advantage of a woman "under the influence" she'd personally hunt him down like a dog and string him up.

After getting over the shock of being threatened by his own grandmother, Nigel had promised she'd never have a reason to go hunting.

A promise to this day he'd never broken.

"Where'd you park?"

Kimberly was taking great care to smooth out some perceived wrinkles in her dress. "Somewhere outside."

Considering there were thousands of cars "somewhere outside" Nigel opted to not worry about hers for the time being. He'd take her home in his Jeep. She could get her car tomorrow.

Fifteen minutes later, they were heading down the Strip in bumper-to-bumper traffic, horns honking, music blasting out of neighboring cars, and Kimberly singing—of all things—old show tunes.

Which might be okay if she could carry a tune.

Or knew the words.

Nigel interrupted a few times to ask directions, and Kimberly, still singing, would cheerfully comply.

Twenty minutes later they arrived at her high-rise and took the elevator to the twenty-first floor.

"Key?" Nigel asked when they reached her door.

"Yes." She grinned.

"Is it in your purse?"

She held her hands over her head. "Maybe it's on me."

Kimberly, playful. Who woulda thought.

"Give me your purse."

With a feigned pout, she relinquished her leather bag.

Fortunately, it was a snap finding her keys because there was so little else in there. A wallet, sunglasses case, several tubes of lipstick, nail file, a tin of breath mints, the notepad, remnants of a granola bar. Unlike his sisters who crammed their bags with so much stuff, it was a miracle they didn't have back problems lugging around those weighty bags.

Nigel extracted the keys, didn't bother asking which one to use because it seemed easier to just test the few she had, and got the door open on the second try.

After ushering her inside, he fumbled along the wall for the light switch and flicked it on.

Her place was what he expected, in a way, and then not. Sure, he figured she made enough money to have nice things, and she did. A pristine white couch with matching side chairs. Gleaming wood floors. Elegant lamps, the kind that cost more than the average person could probably afford.

But there was no life in the room.

Everything neat, laid out as though an interior decorator had said this and that would look fabulous, and Kimberly had gone along with it because she was already halfway out the door with places to go and people to see and lots and lots of work to do.

Kimberly toddled into the room, wisps of her blond hair falling loose.

Rapunzel, Rapunzel, let down your hair.

"You should drink the rest of that water," he said, pointing to the bottle she still carried. He'd also purchased a bag of pretzels and an apple to counterbalance her Cosmopolitan spree. During her medley of rousing musical tunes, she'd munched part of the apple and a few pretzels.

She kicked off one shoe, then the other, mumbling something about whims. When she caught his eye, she dutifully took a sip of water.

Like a little kid. Except he had a feeling she'd never really been one.

"You going to be okay?" he asked, taking a step back to the door. He didn't like leaving her here alone. It seemed such a big, empty place and she looked so small, so lonely in it.

She frowned. "Maybe not."

"Are you feeling sick?"

"No." She walked slowly toward him, never breaking eye contact, not stopping until her chest was right smack up against him. He shuddered a gasp at the feel of her soft, full breasts pressed against his stomach.

She leaned back to look up into his face, wavering a little for balance. He lightly touched her back to steady her, his entire body aching to touch her more even as he knew he couldn't. Wouldn't.

With a playful smile, she jiggled the water bottle.

"Let's pretend we're back on the bridge to Bellagio," she whispered.

8

"PRETEND WE'RE—" Nigel inhaled sharply as Kimberly pressed her body full-length against his, his thoughts obliterated by their body heat, the teasing scent of her.

"On the bridge to Bellagio," she repeated, shaking the water bottle. "You know how it was on the bridge," she whispered, nuzzling her chin against his sternum, "all that surging water and swelling music. The lights, the color, the…"

The word *desire* lit up in his mind like a twenty-foot-high flashing neon sign. When he'd first seen Kimberly on the bridge, looking so luscious in that bright yellow outfit, her face lighting up when she saw him, a fire began to smolder deep and low in his gut.

She sloshed her water bottle again, spilling some on the floor.

If they couldn't even control the water bottle, how were they supposed to control themselves? If she hadn't been drinking, different story. But tonight, no.

He slipped his hands to her shoulders. "Let's not play pretend," he murmured.

"All right, let's play for real."

For real. For keeps. What he'd come to her agency for. And here he was, a little over a week later, wanting those things with this handful who was attempting to merge her body with his, a wicked gleam in her eyes.

God, how he wanted her....

Summoning every shred of willpower, he gently pushed her away as he wavered on the edge of leaving or staying. Staying meant trouble. Best to leave. "You need anything before I go?"

She looked at him, those gray eyes turning dark, foreboding, and for a moment he wondered if she was going to go the route of "no fury like a woman scorned" and demand he leave. For good. And to think only a few hours ago, Genius Boy had sworn to himself that all he wanted was for her to make the first move, and he'd take care of the rest.

Of course, he hadn't counted on pink drinks fuzzying the picture.

"Yes," she suddenly said, a twinkle returning to her eyes. "I need to do something." But before he could respond, she added in a singsong, "Be right back."

"What?" She didn't hear. Too busy traipsing down the hallway, threads of her golden hair tumbling from her rapidly unraveling hairdo.

A door slammed.

Kimberly danced into her bedroom, doing her best slinky moves across the floor because, look out world, she was ready to be the hottest, baddest femme fatale Nigel had ever laid his baby blues on.

If he thought those bimbos at the bar could dress hot, he had another thing coming because Kimberly Logan was going to blow that big ol' luscious bald head's mind!

She staggered to a stop in front of the dresser and asked her reflection, "What mind-blowing, bimbo-competing clothes should I wear?" She thought back to what they'd had on. The tall one hadn't been wearing a bra under her T-shirt.

Kimberly gave her head a toss. "*Pfft.* Braless is nothin'."

The petite one had been wearing a body-hugging orange dress.

"Like that takes imaginashun?" She frowned at her moment of mush-mouth. She hadn't had *that* much to drink. She was fully in control of her faculties, knew exactly what she was doing, and her tongue and lips would just have to get with the program.

Okay, back to the bar broads. The third one had been wearing some leather halter number with her boobs popping out.

Kimberly frowned, straightened. "*I* can pop better than *that*."

Where had she stashed that killer black corset what's-his-name had given her as a gift? Good ol' what's-his-name who seemed to think a racy gift would shift their dating status into high gear? It'd shifted their dating status all right. Into reverse. She'd broken up with him and tossed the lacy, satin-cupped gift into…

Right-o. Dresser. Bottom drawer. Land of the lost clothes. If she remembered correctly, a pair of fishnet stockings were stuffed in there, too.

A few minutes later she was squeezing her body into the cut-high-on-the-thigh black corset with see-through lace panels and underwire satin bra cups that didn't just *promise* cleavage, but *delivered* it. Big time.

She reared back, caught herself on the chair, and checked out her reflection.

"Wow!"

Hell, even *she* was impressed at how much she popped!

"This screams for come-get-me high heels," she muttered, angling herself toward the closet. She was having a little trouble breathing in this body-molding corset, but figured as long as she didn't try to yell or cough, she'd be okay.

A few moments later, after one last look in the mirror, she sauntered out to the living room, ready to play the X-rated version of Bridge to Bellagio.

NIGEL HAD SPENT the past few minutes either wondering what Kimberly was doing or worrying about her. Occasional thumps and mutterings from the bedroom told him she was busy doing something, although exactly what had his mind reeling. He'd toyed with leaving, but every time the thought crossed his mind, he knew he couldn't. For one thing, he didn't want her to walk out and see he'd gone. A gentleman never stranded a lady.

For another, he was concerned for her well-being.

And, last, he cared about her. A lot.

When he'd been in that bar having every guy's wet dream—sexy, hot-and-ready women falling all over him—he couldn't have cared less because all he cared about was one woman. Kimberly.

Cared what she was thinking, what she was doing, when he could quit the crazy game and be with her, just her, again.

Doesn't she realize I love her?

Whoa. He shut his eyes, wondering when he'd crossed that line. *For all my searching for Ms. Right, you'd think I'd have enough sense to pick a woman who also wanted marriage, family.* But no, he'd fallen for a woman who wanted career and…well, career.

And yet when he looked back, he and Kimberly had clicked in a way he never had with another woman. Like that day in her office when she'd snapped that pencil in two and he'd realized that underneath her stylish and armored exterior beat a passionate heart.

Or at the picnic, when she broke through Austin's tough-guy exterior, the same kid Nigel had been working months to get through to. Which showed Nigel her passionate heart was filled with compassion and insight, too.

Or earlier tonight on that bridge, when they first saw each other. He'd never forget how her face lit up when she spied him. The only thing that would have made it perfect was if he could have swept her into his arms, kissed those luscious lips.

A hot ache shot to his groin.

If he didn't cool it with the sweet and yearning thoughts, he'd have his grandmother's ghost hunting him down.

From the bedroom, another thump, followed by a "Wow!"

He scrubbed a hand across his face. *What is she doing?*

Puffing a breath, he sauntered into the living room, knowing the only way to maintain his sanity was to *not* dwell on why Kimberly was thrashing about, alone, in her bedroom.

He stepped off the polished wood floor onto an expansive white rug that seemed to delineate the living room proper. For a woman who obviously liked to wear bright colors, this room was devoid of them. White-covered chairs and couch. Icy blue-gray walls. A nonfunctional ivory hearth topped with a large, square mirror. *Shame. A real fireplace could warm up this space.*

In the midst of this white space were several black accessories. A black side table that held a CD player and speakers, a black stone-top desk dotted with odds and ends, a black chair.

Considering how clean and neat everything looked, he bet she didn't spend much time in here even after she got home.

He walked by the desk, checking out the items on it. A smattering of sticky notes—*those* were in color—with words scribbled on them. Huh. He'd assumed her writing would be as neat and controlled as she was, but apparently not. On the corner of the desk was a crystal vase filled with ivory silk flowers. Next to it, a coffee cup crammed with pens. Coffee cup? He bent over and read the words scripted on its outside. Mornings Are For The Birds.

He imagined a sleepy Kimberly, a robe half wrapped around her, trundling near comatose into the kitchen to make a pot of coffee. He wondered how many cups it took her before she was ready to join the land of the living. Two? Three?

If he were around, he'd encourage her to switch to herbal tea after the first one.

His gaze shifted to a silver-framed photograph of four people—a woman, man and two children.

He picked it up for a closer look.

It was easy to pick out Kimberly with her sunshine-blond hair and big gray eyes. She looked to be around ten, standing next to a woman who had the same blond hair and wore an expression he'd seen once or twice on Kimberly's face. A look of yearning, as though something she wanted was just out of reach.

"That's my family."

Nigel looked up and nearly lost his grip on the frame.

Before him stood Kimberly, dressed like a dominatrix on the make.

His gaze dropped to the spiked heels, crawled up her shapely fishnet-stockinged legs, got momentarily stuck on a patch of creamy skin peeking through black lace. And when he raised his gaze to those black satin cups…

"Uhh…" Words escaped him. Hell, *he* escaped him. His body was in shock, his mind AWOL as he stared at two luscious, cup-runneth-over breasts.

A man needed to be prepared when Pollyanna decided to go to the dark side.

"Kimberly," he choked, his brain cells finally kicking in, "what in the *hell* are you doing?"

She took a deep breath, and for a moment he swore those cups were really going to runneth over.

"All those women were throwing themselves at you."

"What breasts— I mean what women?"

"The ones at the bar."

"Oh, those women." He swallowed, trying to wet his suddenly dry mouth. "They didn't throw themselves at me."

"Yes, they did."

"Okay, they did."

She leaned one nicely rounded hip against the desk. "I didn't want you to go overboard and give my agency a bad name." She swiped back a strand of hair. A lost cause because more of it seemed to be tumbling loose than staying in place.

"So you dress up like this—" he motioned up and down the black-lace-and-satin corset as his pulse lodged somewhere in his esophagus "—to make sure I don't go overboard with another woman? Isn't that the whole point of my joining Life Dates? To be a bad boy and go overboard?"

His grandmother's voice rose from the grave. "I'll hunt you down like a dog...."

"Which I'm not doing tonight," he quickly added.

He rubbed his suddenly sweaty palms down the sides of his pants. "Kimberly, sweetheart, you're not being a success coach right now."

"Yes, I—"

"You're jealous, that's all."

She snorted indignantly. "I'm not jealous."

"That's not a criticism, it's a compliment." His mind was a jumble of heat and words and he should leave, should leave...

She teetered.

"Take off those skyscrapers," he muttered, "before you fall over and break your neck." Just what this evening needed. A rush trip to the emergency room.

She looked down her at her fishnet-stockinged legs, back up. "They're my come-get-me shoes."

Like he needed that comment.

But she didn't argue and kicked them off, in the process stepping even closer. He could look down and see the shadow of her cleavage. And what a lovely cleavage. Dark and inviting between two round scoops of soft, full plumpness....

"Take my jacket," he croaked, slipping out of it in record time and tossing it over her shoulders. Not that it exactly covered what she was wearing, but at least there was less bare skin to taunt him.

She gestured to the photograph he'd been looking at. "That's a picture of my family. The year my mom got sick."

"I'm sorry," Nigel said, his mood sobering.

"It's okay." Kimberly picked up the picture, stared intently at it. "Dad always said I looked just like her." She set the picture back down, turning her attention back to Nigel. "I figure that's why he grew so distant after Mom died. Every time he looked at me, he saw her. Then he turned his back altogether, later, when I disappointed him...."

Her voice trailed off, but not before he heard the catch in it.

His arms wrapped around her, pulling her close. Whatever had happened—and he guessed it had something to do with her riding out of town on a black horse, although there's no way he'd ask about that now—only a coldhearted bastard wouldn't offer comfort. Lightly rubbing her back, he looked out at the sea of black and white in her living room, which suddenly made sense.

This wasn't a home, it was a place to come back to every night. *She's afraid to have a home because it'll go away, in the blink of an eye, the way hers did years ago.*

After cradling her for a while, he said quietly, "I think it's time we call it a night."

"Don't go."

"Kim—"

"Please," she said, leaning back and giving him a pleading look.

When he hesitated, she pressed her forefinger against his lips. "Sounds like yes to me," she whispered before traipsing over to the CD player and slipping in a disk.

Nat King Cole's rich, deep voice started singing "Unforgettable."

"Remember?" Kimberly asked, swaying in place.

Of course. This song had been playing when he'd walked into her office last week, the day after their passionate explosion the night before. "Yes."

"This is the version Nat King Cole's daughter did with him." Kimberly sashayed closer, her arms opened wide, welcoming him into their embrace. "One dance?"

Which he thought about saying no to, until her lips curved into a sweet, imploring smile.

"Just one." Then he'd go.

She sank into his arms and for a moment he froze. But the warning bells in his head subsided as their bodies fell into a comfortable rhythm. He'd never been a dancer, at best he shuffled back and forth, but he could've been Fred Astaire the way she molded herself to him, moving in time.

He glanced over at the mirror above the faux fireplace. He liked how Kimberly's head leaned against his chest, the golden curls barely discernible against his flesh-colored T-shirt. And below the line of his jacket, the teasing glimpse of her legs.

She murmured something.

He pressed his palm against the small of her back, pulling her a little closer. "Yes?"

"I've never gotten swept away like this before. With anyone." She wrapped her arms around his neck and, going up on tiptoe, planted a kiss on his neck.

Heat flamed from that point, crackling like wildfire over the rest of his body. He cradled her head in his hands, wisps of her silky hair teasing his skin. And even as he thought no more, no more, his fingers pulled out a pin, his reward being another golden lock falling loose.

"You should wear your hair loose," he murmured.

"And you," she whispered, stepping back out of his arms, "should bend over."

Just when he thought he'd gotten a handle on Kimberly, she threw him a curveball. "What?"

"My King of Siam, bow to your Anna."

"King of—?"

"Yul Brynner, remember? *The King and I?*"

He recalled her making the reference to *The King and I* in the dressing room, although he'd had no idea what she was talking about at the time. "That's a movie, I take it?"

"Yes," she said, sounding pleased. "He's the pompous, impossibly sexy King of Siam and she's the genteel, but steely, Anna. Yul Brynner played the king in the original movie." She glanced up at his head. "He was bald, too."

"Which made him impossibly sexy?"

"Yes. Just like you."

What man in his right mind wouldn't do a woman's bidding after a line like that?

He leaned over.

Soft, tentative fingers touched his head, lingered, then trailed a path over his skull, down to his ears, back to the crown. "I've wanted to do this again ever since the dressing room," she whispered. She massaged, rubbed, kneaded. Then her fingers slipped down to make slow, lazy little circles on the nape of his neck.

He was conscious of every single spot where her warm fingers touched his flesh. When her hot breath suddenly fanned his scalp, waves of heat radiated over the rest of his skin.

"I should go," he said in a strained voice, starting to straighten.

"Not yet."

He groaned as her lips pressed their velvet warmth against his head. One time. Again. The kisses at first thoughtful, then growing in urgency as her lips dragged across his scalp, stopping here, there. She grew insistent, devouring, the thrill of her exploration sinking hot down to the core of his being.

With great effort, he finally raised his head.

Her lipstick was smeared, her eyes glittering, and in that instant, he swore she was the most alive, sexiest woman he'd ever laid eyes on in his life.

"Anna," he murmured, "the king is ordering you to bed."

WHICH WAS EASIER SAID than done.

After giving him a simmering look, she did that traipsing thing to her bedroom, slinking out of his jacket on the way. At the doorway, she held up the jacket, winked, then dropped it right before she disappeared. The door clicked shut.

He stood in the living room, stunned and hotter than ever after that improvised ministriptease. Those women in the bar were like a pack of Girl Scouts compared to the corseted Kimberly.

He headed toward the closed bedroom door. He'd pick up the jacket, then he'd go.

But as he bent over, she called to him through the bedroom door.

"Nigel?"

"Yes?"

"I can't breathe."

"Why?"

"The corset." A wincing noise. "It's too tight."

He squeezed shut his eyes, fighting the visuals. "Take it off," he croaked.

"Can't." A grunt. "Need your help."

He leaned his head against her door, toying with pounding himself senseless.

"Ouch! I need help!"

As he opened the door, he offered a small prayer to whatever saint helped those in need of emergency willpower.

She lay sideways on her bed, thrashing as she reached behind her and fumbled with the back of her corset. "It's these damn hooks and eyes," she muttered.

He walked to the side of the bed, trying to think of baseball, football, anything other than her pink skin peeking through black lace, the sinful texture of black satin and those awe-inspiring, mind-melting breasts.

"Turn over on your stomach," he rasped.

She did as told, a first.

He leaned over, staring down at the back of the corset and the shiny line of tiny hooks and eyes. Good thing there was ample light in this room as it required a brain surgeon to do this kind of microsurgery. How the hell had she gotten into this thing on her own?

He played with the first hook, his fingers feeling way too big for such intricate, small objects. Miraculously, he opened the first one. Then the second.

By the tenth or twentieth—they were becoming a blur—beads of sweat were forming on his forehead. He grabbed a corner of her sheet and wiped his head.

"Ohh," she murmured against her pillow, "I can breathe again. You're *sooo* good."

He crossed himself, adding a small side-prayer to his grandmother to please not sic the hounds of hell on him, then zeroed in on the next hook and eye.

Finally, finally he popped the last one.

She lay there, the opened corset exposing the taut planes of her back. Just underneath her left shoulder blade was a small, teasing mole.

"Feel better?" He felt like hell.

She wriggled a little. "I can breathe, it's just…" She wriggled again. "Ouch."

"What?"

"Something's poking me in the rib."

"Can you, uh, slip this off now by yourself?"

"Sure." She moved one way, grunted, twisted a little in the other direction.

This went on for a solid minute, punctuated by an occasional "Ouch."

If I leave her like this, she'll hurt herself.

"Here," he said, putting his hands around her waist, "let me help you stand up."

He eased her into a sitting position on the side of the bed. The corset hung loose, her breasts unencumbered, although they weren't one-hundred-percent exposed. Yet. He thought about closing his eyes then realized that would be about the dumbest thing he could do. Fumbling and groping like a blind man wasn't the smoothest approach to the situation.

He took a deep breath, like a diver going into the deep end, and hoisted her to her feet.

He cleared his throat. "Can you get it off now?"

"Uh-huh."

"Is that a yes?"

"Mmm, yes." She flashed him a big pleased-with-herself smile.

He started to speak, then paused. "This whole ouch-I-need-help was just a setup to get me into your bedroom."

She cocked her head, her gray eyes twinkling. "Would I do that?"

He gulped a breath, although it seemed all the air had been sucked out of the room. "I can't take this any further."

She took hold of the corset on either side of the cups and gently pulled down. Her breasts bobbed free, full and creamy, and he nearly wept at the sight.

"Why not?" she asked, tugging the corset lower.

"Because," he croaked, forcing himself to look into her eyes, "you've been drinking."

"*One* Cosmopolitan and I'm turned down?"

"Those were awfully big Cosmopolitans, and you were sucking down your second when I joined you." He closed his eyes, wishing he'd said any word but "sucking."

She tsked. "I have a buzz on, nothing more."

And I have a raging hard-on, nothing less. "The hounds of hell," he murmured hoarsely.

"What?"

He opened his eyes, his mouth salivating at the sight of her gorgeous breasts hanging like ripe fruit over a half-peeled-off corset. He swallowed, hard. "I was brought up to never take advantage of an inebriated woman."

"Well, I'm not inebriated. And to take any worries off your mind…" Her voice dropped to a throaty whisper. "I'll take advantage of you instead." She placed her hands on his biceps and squeezed. "I love how your muscles flex and bunch when you move."

"Thank you. I should go before—"

Her hands slipped down and framed his hard-on through his pants.

"Like you said the other night to me," she whispered, massaging his hard sex through the material, "you worry too much."

He emitted a sound like a wounded animal.

Kimberly laughed softly as she unbuttoned his pants and slowly pulled down the zipper. "I like the lights on," she murmured, "so I can see you."

She opened his pants and tugged them, plus the briefs, down enough to release his rock-hard penis. Pausing, she admired the sight. She'd expected him to be larger than average, but not this big. If she wasn't so curious, and aroused, it could be intimidating.

"*Nice,*" she murmured.

He groaned.

She lightly trailed the tips of her nails slowly down, then back up his thickened length. He was solid and hard underneath a silky-smooth sheath. She circled him with one hand and squeezed.

"You like this?"

A raw sound of pleasure rumbled from deep inside him.

She eased down to a sitting position on the bed, her face level with his sex. Looking up, she met his gaze as she flicked her tongue around the tip of his cock, once. Twice.

"That?"

"Yes," he choked.

She rubbed her face against his erection, feeling its pulsing hardness against her cheek, lips. Then she brought up her other hand and trailed her fingers down his shaft, down to the soft weight of his balls that she gingerly fondled and stroked.

His breath hitched, the tension from his body reverberating through her. "Do you have—?"

"No." Just as the first time had been unplanned, so was tonight. She hadn't thought they'd end up here, and she hadn't carried spares in a long time. She couldn't even remember the last time she'd needed to worry about it, it'd been that long.

But she'd already thought about this, knew what she wanted to do.

She blew lightly on the head of his erection, still cupping his testicles with her hand, all the while watching him. His face was larger than most men, the bones strong, perfectly symmetrical, yet there was something delicate about his features.

No, not delicate. Fearless. He was unafraid to be real, to show his emotions. *That* was his sensitivity. What he called both a curse and a blessing. More the latter, she thought, watching the procession of emotions on his face. Wonder, intensity, desire. Seeing what he felt deepened her connection to him.

"It's my turn to please you," she murmured, enjoying the surge of power it gave her to pleasure him. It had never been like this with a man, the teasing interplay of give and take. Being the giver had a surprising reward. At this moment, she swore his emotions, powerful and raw, penetrated her more profoundly than any physical touch.

She trailed the tip of her tongue along the length of his staff, down and up, relishing his deep-throated groans. Then, again circling him with her hand, she lightly stroked up and down as she took him into her mouth.

He tasted like man and salt as she licked and sucked, her hand increasing its sliding tempo with the rhythm of her tongue and lips. Suddenly, he coiled his hands into her hair, holding her head still as he gently thrust in small, controlled movements.

Her mouth took him in, deeper, as she slid her hands around him and splayed her fingers wide on the cool, naked skin of his buttocks. She pushed lightly, drawing him closer, harder into her mouth. Her breasts tingled at the sound of the air bursting out of his lungs in an agonized moan of pleasure.

Suddenly, his hips froze. He reared back his head, his face dark with his groans. Then with a jerking motion, he released a guttural sound, like a jungle cry. Fierce, loud, prolonged. She held still, feeling his body rushing toward release.

Afterward, he silently sank onto the bed with her and wrapped her in his arms. She rested her cheek against the quieting rise and fall of his chest as he stroked her arms, shoulders, the contours of her face.

Damn, she felt good. And giddy. Of course, next time she wanted to be sure they could make love. To experience, as Maurice had so delicately phrased it, "the whole enchilada." Maybe she should buy one of those economy packs of condoms. They probably contained at least several dozen.

What was she doing?

What had happened tonight was hot and wonderful, but that's all it could be. Another one-nighter. She didn't have time for a relationship. If she let things get out of hand, she'd find herself picking out china patterns instead of focusing on her business.

She bit her bottom lip, hating herself for being…afraid. Okay, she was admitting that was the word. *Afraid.* So what? Maintaining a healthy fear these past few years had kept her safe, in control, admired by her peers and community.

Shifting a little, she turned her back to Nigel who continued to lazily cuddle her. What they shared was fantastic, yes, but she needed to make it clear it wasn't long-term.

Or maybe end it altogether before it got out of hand.

KIMBERLY BLINKED OPEN her eyes, squinting at the too-bright sunlight spearing through her partially open bedroom blinds.

Did I forget to close them when I went to bed?

Frowning, she shut her eyes. *Can't remember.*

Feels hot in here.

Hot. Sun. She peered at the light streaming through the blinds again. *Too early for the sun to be that high.*

With great effort, she rolled over and stared at her clock, piecing together the red digital lines that formed numbers.

9…30?

9:30!

I overslept!

Shit, that advertising meeting is in thirty minutes.

Dragging her fingers through her hair, which got stuck in a wad of pins—*did I forget to brush my hair out last night, too?*—she mentally checked off what she needed to do to get to the office by ten. Oh, God, no way she'd make it by then. The drive alone, at top speed, was a good fifteen minutes. No way she could shower, get dressed, do her hair in the other fifteen.

I'll call Maurice, tell him to stall the TV advertising people. If she hustled, she could be there by ten-thirty. Yes, Maurice would be livid and she'd never hear the end of it, but she'd deal with that later.

She leaned over to grab the phone next to the bed when she spied the corset and fishnet stockings piled on the floor. She paused, remembering slipping them off last night after Nigel fell asleep.

Nigel. Memories of last night seared through her mind.

"Good morning, sleepyhead!" said a familiar male voice. "I made you some wicked java."

She turned to see him walking into the bedroom holding a mug. Her heart lurched. He looked bigger than life and devastatingly handsome in those khaki pants and body-hugging T-shirt. Put a gold earring on him and he'd look like a bad-boy Mr. Clean.

He stopped next to the bed and grinned. "Mornin', beautiful." He handed her the mug. "Two Skinny Sweets, right?"

"Right," she mumbled, accepting the coffee, salivating at the roasted scent. This was nice, this coffee in bed stuff. "Do me a favor and call Maurice? Tell him I'll be in by ten-thirty?"

"No problem. I can get you to work by then."

Right, the Jeep. Nice, that getting-a-ride-home stuff.

She spied a red streak behind his ear. "Did you cut yourself?"

He ducked to look in the dressing-table mirror. "Oh, thought I'd washed them all off."

"Washed what off?"

"Your kisses."

A hazy memory of caressing and kissing his head sharpened in her mind. Everything that had happened last night had been hot, electric and satisfying in a way she'd never experienced before.

He was turning her world upside down. Making her crazy with desire one moment, cozy and content the next. Can't make this into a relationship. Can't. Can't.

Nigel frowned. "You okay?"

She blinked, blew some steam off her coffee. "Fine. Just worried about getting into work late. Big meeting this morning."

"Don't sweat it, sweetheart," he murmured, laying a big, warm hand on her shoulder. "I'll get you there by ten-thirty."

Nice, this too-good-to-be-true-man stuff.

9

MAURICE TAPPED HIS PEN impatiently against the surface of his teak desk, staring at Kimberly with that you're-late-again look she'd come to know too well.

"I'm sorry," she said with a sigh, glancing in the mirror over the guest couch to ensure she looked put together for today's meeting with Barnet and Owens, the advertising agency that was pitching the TV campaign idea for Life Dates.

She unbuttoned her jacket so the new blouse she purchased last week—an impulse buy, something she seemed to be doing more often lately—was better seen. She'd liked its dancing shoes and hats design, which she thought made her look less regimented. She touched her pearl-drop earrings, recalling Nigel checking to make sure she had both on before they'd left her place earlier.

He'd also stared oddly at her lips, murmuring something about her lipstick being on too perfectly.

"It's ten twenty-nine," Maurice said.

"I said I'd be here by ten-thirty," she shot back, "and I am." Although she really couldn't blame Maurice for being uptight this morning. This meeting was his brainchild, and a damn good one, too, because TV was a critical marketing step for Life Dates. "Sorry."

"Apology accepted," he said. "Anyway, not such a big deal you're late as Angie, one of the ad team, had to return to her car for a laptop. She'll be back in a minute." Maurice joined Kimberly where she stood on the Oriental rug and glanced at their reflections. He straightened his tie, a skinny silver one that complemented his formfitting, charcoal suit.

"New suit?" she asked.

"Helmut Lang knockoff." He gave Kimberly a once-over. "You look different, dear."

"You've seen this suit before."

"Yes, and the shoes and the chignon and the pearl earrings, but something about you looks *different*."

At that moment the door swung open and in strolled Nigel.

"He, uh, gave me a ride to work," she murmured.

Maurice flashed her a so-*that's*-why-you-look-different look.

"Good morning, Mr. Durand," Maurice said. "Nice to see you again." He peered at a spot on Nigel's head. "Did you cut yourself?"

Nigel swiped at a spot behind his ear.

"No, more toward the crown," Maurice said, stepping closer and gesturing to the spot. "Looks more like lip—"

"Thanks," Nigel said, doing a global swipe of his head. "Thought I'd gotten them all."

"*All?*" Maurice slid a you-wild-woman-you glance at Kimberly.

Which she pretended not to see as she crossed to the desk and tossed back a few yogurt-soy thingies.

"Sorry there was no time for breakfast," Nigel said, watching her reach for a second handful. "Since today's my picnic with Austin, and you said you'd like to join us, how 'bout I pick you up at noon? Afterward, I'll drop you off at your car."

Austin. She'd almost forgotten. "I don't know how long this meeting will be...."

The door whooshed opened and in walked a thirtysomething woman—the kind Kimberly called "professional razzle-dazzle" because of her make-it-happen presence, upscale suit, designer briefcase.

Spying Kimberly, Razzle Dazzle made a beeline to her. "I'm Angie Canavesio," she said with a smile, her teeth so white they could be worn on a necklace. "Pleasure to meet you." As they shook, she continued, "Sorry I held things up, but it was imperative I retrieve the laptop for today's presentation." Her gaze drifted to Nigel and her hazel eyes widened slightly.

"This is Nigel Durand," Kimberly said.

"Yes, I recognized you," Angie said, her all-business tone going a little breathy.

"Shall we begin the meeting?" Kimberly said, fighting a surge of green-eyed monster and not liking it one bit.

"Yes, you should," Maurice said, shuffling some papers. "Because Ms. Logan has a lunch appointment at noon."

AN HOUR AND TWENTY MINUTES later, Angie was wrapping up the PowerPoint presentation at the glass circular table in a corner of Kimberly's office. Next to Angie sat an older gentleman named Carl Mitchell, who'd introduced himself as an advertising manager at Barnet and Owens. Next to Carl sat a twentysomething named Luke Glaser, who was part of the "creative team."

"At the end of the TV spot…" Angie said, tapping a button on the keyboard. On the computer monitor was a picture of a TV screen displayed with a phone number and Web site address flashing in bold red letters, "…we drive home the selling points with a dynamic call to action." She hit another button and the screen cleared. Angie folded her hands in front of her and flashed that megawatt smile at Kimberly. "Our expectation is a fifteen to twenty-five percent increase in your customer base within the first month alone."

With that kind of growth, Kimberly could bring Maurice on as an associate, something she'd been thinking about lately, hire a new receptionist, eventually move into a bigger office space.

"I like it," she said. "I also like how you hit on a key marketing niche, the night-owl casino workers who'll be watching TV in the early-morning hours." This kept with Kimberly's goal to cater exclusively to Las Vegas singles. Great Dates, on the other hand, offered matching services to anyone, anywhere, which stretched them thin and weakened what they offered locally.

"A lower-priced time slot for TV ads, as well," chimed in Carl.

"Good, good." Kimberly paused. "I just think Vegas singles are more accustomed to flash, and unfortunately, your pitched ideas are…"

Angie nodded. "Boring."

Kimberly paused, liking Angie's no-nonsense summation. "Well, yes."

Angie leaned forward, her chipper attitude shifting into a dead-on serious one. "I have a killer idea." She glanced at the men. "We haven't had a chance to discuss it, but trust me, it's dynamite."

Angie reminded Kimberly of herself when she first launched her business. Gutsy, sparking with ideas, unafraid to turn on a dime.

"Your idea?" Kimberly prompted.

"Well," Angie said, her hazel eyes glittering. "A local celebrity in the ad would pull in viewers. Leave Great Dates eating your local dust. When I walked into your lobby and saw The Phantom…" She looked at her co-workers. "You know who he is, right?"

Carl frowned. "The wrestler?"

Angie nodded. "I thought back to that commercial he was in a few years ago."

"The Crusher," murmured Kimberly.

Angie pointed a peach-tipped nail at her. "I bought one of those trucks."

"As did thousands of other women."

"So you're getting my drift. Let's put aside the safe approach and go for what's happening in Vegas—a return to brazen." Angie stood, walked slowly around the table as she spoke.

"Let's face it. Vegas's family-friendly image with its roller coasters and arcades isn't as financially viable as businesses had hoped. Tame fun is on its way out and lustier amusements—the kind that built Vegas—are back in. Like that ad says, 'what happens here stays here.' Your TV ad should reflect this, too. That automobile company no longer makes The Crusher, so those commercial tapes are gathering dust on a shelf somewhere. I'll call our lawyers, get them to negotiate our using a still, maybe a short clip. Women will drool over The Phantom, men will want to be like him, and you'll have both sexes pounding on Life Dates' door. You'll be more successful than you've ever dreamed."

Success. Money. Everything Kimberly had been working toward. But Nigel hated that Crusher commercial, said it was the one thing he'd regretted doing. Kimberly shifted in her seat. "I don't know."

Angie pressed both palms flat on the table as she leaned toward her. "Kimberly, small businesses are going out of business every day because of big-chain conglomerates. You need to push the envelope or your business will be swallowed up by Great Dates."

Kimberly soundlessly tapped the toe of her foot against the carpeting. "Can't we get another celebrity?"

"Sure. But would he—or she—fit the bill? The Phantom is *perfect*." Angie paused. "He is…just a friend, right?"

When Kimberly didn't answer, Angie looked at her co-workers, then back to her.

"Not that I'm one to talk morals in a town like Vegas," Angie said, lowering her voice, "but if he's more than a friend, it could look, well, awkward at best. You've built a reputation as an aboveboard, classy dating service. If people see an ad starring you and your boyfriend the beefcake—sorry, but that's how people would see it—it'll add a salacious slant to the ad. Not that Sin City would be shocked, but you need to be aware of the kind of market that would attract."

It all came back to her reputation. With a sickening realization, Kimberly saw her past creeping up on her. All these years of reinventing herself as a solid citizen of the community running a highly reputable and successful business would crash. She'd be viewed as a charlatan, a joke.

A dirty joke.

She cleared her throat, put on her best professional face. "He's just a client. No more, no less than dozens of others."

As Angie and her co-workers smiled and nodded, Kimberly told herself it wasn't really a lie. After all, he was a client. And, technically, they didn't know what they were beyond that.

"Excellent," Angie said, shutting down her computer. "I'll contact our lawyers as soon as I get back to the office about our rights to the footage."

"Let me check with Nigel about that first," Kimberly suddenly said. It tempered her guilt, a little, if she asked him first about using it, explained how its use meant her fulfilling a years-long dream of success.

Really, the only ethical decision he'd have to make was whether to keep their relationship a secret, not whether to use the footage.

"I SHOULD'VE ASKED if you wanted turkey," said Nigel as he laid out their sandwiches on the picnic table at Doolittle Park. The scents of the desert—warm, earthy—wafted in with passing breezes. Children's squeals could be heard from a nearby playground.

Kimberly studied Nigel as he fussed over where to put the plastic forks, napkins. He was dressed in a pair of shorts and a yellow tank top that consisted of so little material, it was functionally useless as a piece of clothing.

Underneath the tank top, she spied the ridges of his beautifully sculpted abdomen. And above, where his chest was exposed, she had an eyeful of dark chest hair over well-defined muscle.

She shivered in reaction, and he looked over.

"Don't tell me you're cold with that jacket on."

Ask him about the commercial. "N-no." *I'll ask him*

later. Which was the inner dialogue she'd been having with herself ever since he'd picked her up for lunch. She needed her wits about her when she asked, which she didn't have with his bad-boy self dressed like this. Plus, Austin would be showing up any moment and she wanted to discuss the ad with Nigel in private.

Although, if she were totally honest with herself, she knew she was working harder to avoid the discussion than to face it. And if she'd made the right decision about the ad, why was she stalling?

"Hungry?"

She nodded.

"About time you admitted you have an appetite," he teased, nudging her sandwich closer.

He's a natural caretaker. And here I've told him to not bake brownies or wait by the phone anymore.

For a moment, Kimberly wondered if she'd done the wrong thing with this man by fitting him into her six-step bad-boy program. He was kind, honest, loved to pamper a woman, was eager to settle down and have a family. His biggest fault when it came to love was he'd pursued the wrong women.

Which really came down to what one thought of oneself. By listening to some of her motivational tapes, he could probably learn more about healthy choices than her forcing him to dress, act and woo like a bad boy.

Maybe, when she talked to him about the commercial, she'd suggest this approach instead. That could be a win-win. *Do the commercial, and let's simplify the whole Life Dates experience.*

The commercial. She shifted and reshifted her feet under the table, not liking the growing niggling doubts she had every time she thought about it.

"You seem worried," he said, setting one of the soda cans on a stack of paper napkins so they wouldn't blow away.

"Maybe."

"Want to talk about it?"

The hiss of tires on sand diverted their attention. They watched Austin ride his bike up to the table.

"Later," murmured Kimberly, "when we're alone."

Nigel nodded, mouthed, "He's on time," his eyes shining with surprise and pride.

Lunch was a lot livelier than the week before. Oh, Austin had his in-your-face moments, like the time Nigel asked if the boy was still getting a tattoo and Austin whipped out a colorful picture of a pirate he'd drawn, saying this was what the tattoo would look like and if somebody—Nigel, no doubt—didn't like it, tough. Kimberly was impressed with Nigel's reaction. He quietly changed topics, kept the conversation upbeat. Austin eventually cooled down, talked about acing a math quiz, mentioned a girl who'd invited him to a school dance.

"She cute?" asked Nigel.

Austin nodded, taking a bite of his sandwich.

"You going to the dance?" asked Nigel.

Austin shrugged, dipped his head. He started to wipe his mouth with the back of his hand, paused, reached for a napkin. "What about you two?" he asked.

"What about us?" asked Nigel.

"You two dating or what?"

Nigel took a long slug of his drink while Kimberly darn near inhaled the rest of her coleslaw.

"I'd like to date her," Nigel finally said, breaking the silence, "but she's not so sure."

Kimberly smiled awkwardly as Austin's dark eyes surveyed her face.

"What's up with that?" he asked.

It suddenly felt as though she'd been stuck under a bank of interrogation lights. She flapped open her jacket, debating whether to just take the damn thing off or sweat to death. *Too much thinking.* She slipped off the jacket, relishing the feel of cooling air against her heated skin.

"We're… I'm… Can we put this topic on a back burner?" Avoiding their gazes, she folded her jacket on the bench seat next to her.

"Let's not put her on the spot, Austin. I'm still wooing her to my way of thinking."

Austin grinned. "Sorry."

"Speaking of putting people on the spot," Nigel continued, his voice low, thoughtful, "I want to apologize for doing that to you." He paused, meeting Austin's gaze. "I've seemed to think that being a good mentor means telling you what's best for you, when what's more important is to listen better, understand where you're coming from."

A look of surprise skittered across Austin's face. "Like telling me I should try out for soccer?"

"Like that."

Austin rubbed his finger along the dark indentations of long-ago carved initials in the wooden table. "Not sure if I will."

Nigel picked up the last of his sandwich. "I support whatever decision you make."

After a drawn-out moment, Austin downed the rest of his soda, stood. "Gotta go. Can't be late for wood shop."

"Wood shop?" Nigel did a double take. "Didn't know you were taking that class."

"I'm not." Austin picked up his bike, swung his leg over the seat and plopped down on it. "Patty is. I walk her to her next class."

"She's the girl who asked you to the dance?" asked Nigel.

Austin grinned, tapping his foot against the pedal. "Yeah," he muttered before starting to ride off.

A few feet away, he stopped. "Hey," he called over his shoulder, looking at Kimberly. "You should go out with him."

10

Steps four and five: Kiss her 'til she whimpers, love her 'til she screams

FIFTEEN MINUTES LATER, Nigel opened the sunroof on the Jeep. Sunshine poured in, warming his skin. "Ever seen the Valley of Fire?"

"No," Kimberly answered.

He twisted the key in the ignition and the motor growled to life. He waited for a car to pass, then pulled out onto Mead Street. "Want to be spontaneous?"

She gave him a double take. "Right this moment?"

"Yes."

"No."

"Adventurous?"

"No."

He chuckled, slowing to a red light. "Now, why doesn't that surprise me?"

With a small huff, she rolled back her shoulders. Quite a feat considering she had that seat belt strapped on tighter than a straitjacket.

Speaking of jackets, he was glad she hadn't put back on the one to her suit, although he'd watched her mentally debate whether to for a solid minute after they'd returned to the Jeep from their picnic with Austin. Instead of mentioning it was too warm for a jacket, Nigel had kept his mouth shut. Thanks to Kimberly, he was learning that imposing his opinion wasn't always the smoothest approach.

His reward for being, well, *un*imposing was that she looked very pretty in that blouse with its playful pattern of green and pink shoes and hats. *Playful.* The way she'd acted last night, too, although it'd taken one big mutha Cosmopolitan to get her there.

He hoped she could be that way naturally, too.

"Maurice said you didn't have any other appointments this afternoon," he said casually.

"Since when do you and Maurice discuss my appointments?"

The light changed and he shifted into first. "We don't," he said, pretending not to hear the suspicion in her voice. "He just mentioned it when I returned to pick you up." Actually, after Nigel had said he had the afternoon free, Maurice suddenly made a few phone calls, *then* mentioned Kimberly had no more appointments for the day.

"So," Nigel continued, "want to go?"

Pause. "Go where?"

"Valley of Fire."

"I can't."

"Ever been there?"

"No, but—"

"It'll take your breath away. I've never understood

why tourists fly hundreds of miles to see the glitzy Strip yet never check out one of the most awe-inspiring natural sites in the state, less than an hour away. In a couple of months, when temperatures turn crispy, we'll be shake and bakes driving out there with the sunroof open. But a beautiful, breezy day like today? Now's our chance."

She gave a shake of her head. "As I said—"

"Yes, I know. You can't. Or you won't?"

From the corner of his eye, he saw her smooth a hand down her skirt, as though ironing out her thoughts. "I should go back to the office. I have paperwork to catch up on, calls to make, and while we're there, I'd like to discuss something with you."

"We're talking now."

"It's a business issue."

"Business?" He grunted. "Tell you what. Play hooky with me and we can talk business later. But not this afternoon."

He punched a button on the CD player. Soft, seductive music mixed with the swirl of breezes. A wistful voice, the trickle of piano keys.

"You listen to Norah Jones?" Kimberly asked.

"I like her music."

"I should've known." She brushed back a wind-blown strand of hair. "You like Celine Dion, too."

"Hey, just because I can look and act bad doesn't mean the sensitive guy died." He glanced at Kimberly's sensible skirt and matching sensible pumps, and thought how last night she was anything but sensible. He'd love to see that brazen, devil-may-care side of her again. "You of all people should know the outside doesn't always reflect what's inside."

Norah filled the quiet moments that followed as they drove down a street lined with palm trees and ranch-style homes. A group of teenagers, a few coupled off with their arms slung around each other, meandered down the sidewalk. Someone must have told a joke, because the group suddenly erupted in laughter, the lighthearted sound lingering in the air as the Jeep proceeded down the street.

"Reminds me how my kid sisters and their friends used to act," Nigel said. "Having a good time doing nothing. Funny how many of us lose that when we grow up."

After a moment, warm fingers lightly tapped his arm.

He looked over. "I can be spontaneous and adventurous," Kimberly said stiffly.

He grinned, knowing he'd be a very wise man not to mention this was supposed to be a *fun* decision, not a painful one. But considering she'd opted to shuck her jacket, and agreed to do something spontaneous, well, Kimberly Logan was on her way to being a sort of bad girl out to have a good time.

"Great. Let's play hooky."

"YOU'RE RIGHT," Kimberly whispered, "it's awe inspiring."

Nigel shifted down, slowing the Jeep on the road

threading through the Valley of Fire's red-dipped terrain of strangely shaped rocks and jagged sandstone cliffs. The sunroof was still open. When they'd entered the park, he'd insisted they open both their passenger windows, too, to take in the desert breezes.

Kimberly had loosened her seat belt and scooted forward on her seat to view the fierce beauty of the state park. The sun and wind had heightened her color, unraveled wisps of her golden hair. The normally put-together Ms. Logan was looking deliciously unkempt.

"This land," she suddenly said, "makes me think of Austin."

"Because it's wild with lots of attitude?"

"No, silly," she said with a roll of her eyes, "because he loves color. Did you check out the picture he drew of that pirate?"

"Did you check out how I bit my tongue and didn't say one word about no tattoos?" He pointed to an outcropping of layered rock. "Petrified sand dunes. At least a hundred and fifty million years old."

"Amazing," she murmured. "Makes one feel rather insignificant in the grand scheme of things."

"Or realize the importance of the moment."

"Which brings me back to our discussion," she said, turning back to Nigel. "Austin likes to draw. Or paint. Not sure what medium, but he has a raw talent that's begging to be nurtured."

Nigel grew quiet, thinking back to the tough kid who stole those kitschy paintings. A police report had described them as colorful, amateur art.

The colorful part suddenly made sense.

"Ms. Logan, I think you just supplied the missing piece to a puzzle." He told her about Austin's past as a thief who had a taste for expensive electronic equipment and questionable paintings. No one, from the victims to the judge, could fathom why this punk kid had risked being caught, midcrime, to steal Granny So-and-So's smudged pastel or Mr. X's abstract oil.

"You should take him to a museum," Kimberly mused, "and sign him up for a painting class. Bet he'd love it. Bet he'd also stop needling you about another tattoo."

"Advice taken," Nigel said, turning down a side road. He slowed as a tumbleweed rolled lazily across the asphalt in front of the Jeep. "You have good insights into people. Ever think about being a shrink?"

"A long time ago. When I was a psychology major in college, before I dropped out."

"You? The driven businesswoman, a former dropout?"

She shrugged. "Maybe our defeats shape us more than our successes."

He waited for her to say more, but she'd turned away, absorbed once again in the landscape.

A few minutes later, Nigel drove up a brief incline to a parking area and stopped. This was the spot he'd been wanting to take her. His favorite lookout point. The desert stretched out for miles, the horizon a jagged line of red against an endless sky. On a clear day, the blue waters of Lake Mead were visible to the east.

"This is incredible," Kimberly enthused, unsnapping her seat belt. "What's it called?"

"Nigel's Spot," he said, unfastening his. When she shot him a look, he grinned. "I gave it that name."

"Gee, I would never have guessed." A smile crept to the corners of her lips. "So you come here often?"

"And here you told me to can the clichés."

She laughed. "Seriously, now."

"Seriously, several times a year. When the sun goes down, the rocks glow a deep red. Sometimes I imagine the color pulsing, as though it's the earth's heart."

"You bake brownies *and* you're a poet?" Kimberly's eyes twinkled. "Add that bad-boy look and act, and you're definitely a catch, Nicky."

"Nicky, is it?"

His teasing faded as their gazes locked, neither looking away. Here they were in the Valley of Fire, his favorite getaway, and yet staring into those sweet luminous gray eyes he'd grown to adore, and how they looked back at him with such undisguised yearning, had to be one of the more pleasurable sights in his life.

He lowered his gaze to her lips, the soft curve of her breasts, the way her small fine-boned hands curled in her lap. He suddenly felt his size, how big he was next to her, and he didn't want to make the wrong move. This morning when she'd woken up, she'd seemed hesitant. As though she wasn't sure about them.

"Are you using the name Nicky to distance yourself from me?" An awkward question. He really wanted to know if he was reading her signals correctly. More than anything he wanted to kiss her again.

Her gaze drifted slowly, heatedly, over him. "I get confused, but when we're near each other like this..."

He moved closer, sliding his arm along the bucket seat behind her head, letting his fingers graze lightly across the soft skin of her neck. She tilted back her head, rubbing her cheek against his forearm, her eyes filled with a gentle coaxing.

"Kimberly," he murmured, loving the way her name felt in his mouth. Warm and precious.

He reached for the tip of a pin sticking out of the last coil of hair at the nape of her neck and slowly withdrew it, savoring a tumble of hair. He leaned closer—so close he could feel the heat from her skin, smell that hothouse perfume—and burrowed his face in the impossibly silky strands and inhaled deeply.

"Rapunzel, Rapunzel," he whispered hotly in her ear.

She released a small shudder, then murmured, "You're both."

He pulled back. "What?"

"Nigel *and* Nicky," she said with a smile. The warmth in her eyes shifted to raw heat, her voice dropped low. "You're too good to be true, and yet when the mood hits, you can be so wickedly bad." She shuddered a release of breath, her eyes darkening. "I wish we'd planned this better...."

He knew what she meant.

"Hold that thought." He reached over and unlatched the glove compartment. Shoving aside some papers, he pulled out a foil wrapper and waggled it at her.

"So you planned a Jeep tryst?" she teased.

"No," he said, setting the wrapper on the dash. "I bought some and put a few in here so wherever we might end up, your place or mine, we'd have protection." He shot her a look. "Although, if you're in the mood for a Jeep tryst..."

She placed her hands on his chest, pressing her palms against the hardened contour of his pecs. "Nigel," she whispered, clutching the fabric in her fists and drawing him closer, "hold that thought. Hold it real tight."

His fingers tangled in the back of her hair and he leaned close, wanting to take this slow, fighting to rein in his need. Sunlight fell golden on her sweet face, her pink lips parted, and he wanted nothing more than to be lost in her.

His mouth brushed her lips, and when she opened hers wider, inviting him in, he groaned as his tongue thrust deep into the moist warmth.

A thousand feelings flooded Kimberly from all the places he was touching—his hand at her neck, his lips on hers, his thigh pressed against hers. She was vaguely aware of his shirt still fisted in her hands, as though that could anchor her in this sensual onslaught, and fully aware she didn't give a damn.

She wanted him.

Angling her head, she crushed her lips to him, taking him, heat and tension coiling tight inside her. She could devour him right here, oblivious to the world outside, the vast red world of petrified life. She was alive, here, now, and with every cell of her being, she wanted to make love to this man.

Her hands roamed over his broad, muscled shoulders, down across the springy hair that crept over the top of his tank top.

Too much material.

She yanked at the fabric tucked into the waistband, gratified when it sprang loose from his trunks, and dived her hands under to feel his naked chest. Big, hairy, chiseled. She groaned with the sheer pleasure of feeling him.

She tugged open her blouse. Buttons popped.

He paused, looked out the back window. "Nobody for miles," he murmured, before peeling off his tank top and tossing it into the back seat.

Heaving breaths, they paused to look at each other.

Looking at his bronze skin, carpet of chest hair and solid muscle, she licked her lips, feeling ravenous. Insatiable.

He leaned forward, unclasped her bra.

"Come to papa," he murmured, his eyes glittering as he stroked and kneaded her mounds. Taking his smooth head in her hands, she directed it toward her aching breasts. With a growl, he did her bidding, his tongue flicking one nipple, then the other, before his mouth curled around one hardened tip and suckled.

She gasped a sharp breath of pleasure. His mouth was a wonder. He licked, nibbled, withdrew. Over and over, teasing her, until she didn't think she could bear the sweet torture.

"I...want...you..." She writhed on the seat, her body on fire. She grabbed the hem of her skirt, tugged.

Big hands gripped her shoulders, halting her. Smoldering blue eyes met hers.

"Are we going too fast?"

"Are...you...crazy?" she said between ragged pants. Every hot moment they'd shared had led up to this. No way she was denying herself now.

"Please," she urged, damn near delirious with need. "Now."

She toed off her shoes and raised her thighs as he shoved the fabric up to her waist. Desire crackled along on her skin like a spreading blaze.

She looked down at her lower body encased in panty hose, her mound of pale curls pressed underneath sheer beige nylon. She'd been in such a rush this morning, she'd forgotten to put on any panties.

Panting for air, aching for release, she braced her right foot on the dashboard, some dull part of her fevered mind thinking if she shifted a little and rolled the hose off the other leg, no, if she shifted *this* way and pulled the nylon down...

"Hold still, baby."

Nigel's big hands captured the stretched material

between her legs and tugged. It tore apart with an elongated ripping sound.

"Yes," she breathed, the word catching in her throat as she realized he was naked. During her bracing and twisting, he'd slipped off his shorts and briefs and it was all she could do to not salivate at the sight. Those familiar ridges of muscles, dark curly hair sweeping in all the right places and the biggest, hardest…

"Where's the—?" she said on a moan.

He plucked it off the dash, ripped it open. Slipping it on, he looked her over. "Gorgeous," he breathed, the word like a prayer. Then, easing himself over the console, he positioned himself between her legs.

Instinctually, she braced both soles against the dashboard, levering herself as he lowered himself to her.

For a moment, he paused, looking down at her, emotion filling his eyes. "Kimberly, I love you."

"Nigel, I…" Her eyes moistened as a ripple of understanding passed through her heart. All her worries and concerns had been nothing more than the last death throes of an old fear. She was ready, and unafraid, to risk her heart with this man.

"I love you, too," she whispered.

Burying her face against his chest, she wrapped her arms around him and rubbed her hands down his back to his bare hips. Opening herself wider to him, she pressed him closer.

She gasped with the delicious shock of his shaft parting her, sinking into her.

"Look at me," he whispered.

She leaned back her head, meeting his gaze. He pressed deeper as his mouth came down hard on hers, swallowing her cries of pleasure. Her body crumbled around him as he moved inside her with long, hard strokes. She rhythmically urged him on, her body straining for more, greedy for release.

A strangled cry escaped her as she tumbled over the edge, exploding from the inside out, her climax rolling through her in exquisite, sharp contractions.

He suddenly stilled. Then, with a wild, savage sound, his magnificent body shuddered and he drove deep into her, one last final time as he cried out her name.

The world slowly returned to its normal state. He scattered soft kisses on her hair, her face as desert breezes cooled their sweat-drenched bodies. He started to break their body contact, but she held him close.

"Not yet," she whispered, savoring the sensation of his heartbeat against hers. She glanced out her window at the ancient, rugged terrain. Words she hadn't allowed herself to think in years floated through her mind.

Forever.

Eternity.

She welcomed the destiny she shared with this man in her arms.

11

Step six: Pick "The One"

"THOUGHT YOU WERE mostly doin' your kitchen in that country style," Rigo said, turning his head this way, then that, as he stared at the newly installed polished brass faucet in Nigel's sink.

"I am." Nigel set a bowl of chips and salsa on his butcher-block kitchen table. He paused, scrutinized its dents and scratches from years of use. Time to buy a new one.

"Which country?" asked Rigo. "England? This brass faucet looks pretty fancy."

"Nigel Country."

Rigo guffawed, his brown face creased with a wide smile. "Man, that's right. You've been lookin' pretty fancy lately, too, wearing those muscle Ts and gimme-lovin' jeans." His dark eyes twinkling, he reached for a chip. "Does your fashion makeover have anything to do with Ms. Royal Plum?"

It took Nigel a moment, then he remembered. Last time Rigo had been here, there'd been paint chips scattered around Nigel's kitchen. Rigo had teased him about the color Royal Plum, both of them knowing Rigo was referring to something else. A woman. Namely Kimberly, although Rigo didn't know that was her name.

Oh, yeah, Nigel remembered well that evening because he hadn't been in the best of moods. Just a few hours earlier he'd had an exhilarating *and* disastrous encounter with Kimberly that had ended like a Samoan Drop after she'd suddenly dressed, announcing she had to go home. He'd sat there alone after that, uncertain what he'd done wrong and certain she'd walked out of his life for good.

Fortunately, the state of their relationship had turned one-eighty since then.

While playing hooky this afternoon, they'd admitted their feelings. They were in love.

A passionate image of Kimberly swept through his mind. Blond hair sweeping across her flushed face, gray eyes glittering with need. He thought of her climaxing, the way her breath caught and her body tensed. Her hunger for him had been as powerful as his for her. If he'd had his way, he'd have buried his aching body into her deeply, over and over for hours, until neither one of them could walk for a week.

A suggestion he'd whispered after dropping her off at her car.

But after several lingering kisses, she'd begged off, saying she needed to go home and hit the sack early for once this week. That's when he'd asked her out on a real date—no more bad boy and success-coach stuff—and she'd said yes.

He'd liked that. A simple yes. No rules, no games, just yes.

"Yes," he said, opening the refrigerator, "it's Royal Plum I'm looking so fancy for. Juice or *cerveza?*"

"Juice. Just finished my workout."

As Nigel poured apple juice into a glass, Rigo leaned against the kitchen counter and gave his friend an appraising look. "I think my friend will soon be joining the old man's club, eh?"

Pouring a second glass of juice for himself, Nigel grinned, thinking that wasn't such a bad idea. His next step, if he remembered correctly, was picking "The One" and he liked the idea of broaching that topic with Kimberly as soon as possible. They'd both been tumbling about in their solitary worlds long enough. He was tired of wasting time looking, dating and struggling through all the near misses when the answer was right in front of him.

"Who're you calling old?" Nigel handed his friend a glass.

"You, old man."

"Younger than you."

Rigo guffawed. "Not if your Royal Plum *chica* wears you out too much."

Nigel started to toss out a comeback, then stopped.

For the first time, he let Rigo have the last word.

LATER THAT EVENING, Kimberly looked at herself in her bedroom mirror. Her hair was loose and wild, she'd misbuttoned her blouse and her skirt was wrinkled like an accordion. But best of all was the sleepy, contented look on her face.

I look like one wanton, satisfied woman.

After a sassy two-step to the bed, she plopped down and tugged off her air-conditioned panty hose, shivering pleasurably at the memory of Nigel ripping them apart earlier at the Valley of Fire. They'd been as wild and primal as the desert that surrounded them. Tiny fingers of flame skittered over her skin as she recalled their fiery-hot passion, as red as the terrain.

After stripping off her clothes, she headed to the bathroom for a long hot bath. Something steamy, scented with that almond bath oil that had been sitting in her cabinet gathering dust because she always felt too busy to take some time for herself at the end of the day.

She'd been sitting too long, gathering dust.

Today, she decided, was the beginning of a new Kimberly Logan, a woman who had a career *and* a personal life. One she wanted to share with Nigel.

An hour later, she finished toweling off and wrapped her favorite pink chenille robe around her. Famished, she trundled into the kitchen to nosh on leftover Chinese.

Two empty cartons of Chinese food later, she headed back to her bedroom, checking a wall clock on the way. Nine o'clock. Unbelievable, she was ready to go to bed before midnight. *This* was a first. She even had the urge to sit next to the phone and wait for his call, the very thing she'd once lectured him not to do. At this rate, she'd be trying her hand at baking brownies, too.

Me, baking? The concept could make Betty Crocker roll in her grave.

Typically, Kimberly was getting her second wind about now, plunking down at the computer to check a report or e-mail a client. No way tonight. She was tired, sated in more than one way, and couldn't wait to hit the sack.

Couldn't wait to dream of Nigel.

She pulled off her robe, welcoming the onslaught of cool air against her skin. *I'm like a goofy teenager. Daydreaming about this special guy. Next I'll be writing his name in my notebook, over and over, practicing all the ways to write Mrs. Kimberly Durand.*

She paused. Mrs. Kimberly Durand.

I've crossed a lot of lines lately. Am I ready to cross that one into happily-ever-after?

She debated if she should put on the brakes, reel her thoughts back in. After all, this was the man who wanted the picket fence, the two-point-five kids, probably a dog named Scooter.

She met her gaze in the mirror. "You want all that?"

After a beat, she whispered, "Maybe."

Her heart raced, her toes patterned a happy dance against the hardwood floor, and she gave in to the fact she was stupid, immature, head-over-heels, gaga in love.

She hadn't felt this way in years. Ten to be exact, but this time it was different. Better. *Way* better. She wasn't the hormone-crazed teenager who fell for the guy who turned her world upside down. Well, she was still hormone crazed, but this time with a man who she knew in her heart would protect her, love her, ensure her world kept spinning on its axis.

She crossed to her bed and slipped between the cool sheets, the sensation excruciatingly sensual against her flesh. She caught the scent of sweet almond oil on her body and wished Nigel were here to fulfill those heated promises he'd whispered into her ear earlier. She was going to hold him to those promises the next time she saw him.

She released a deep, pleasurable sigh. Oh, yes, that's exactly how they'd end their next "real" date.

Snuggling under the covers, she reached over and flipped off the light. Lying in the dark, she listened to the communion of crickets against the distant buzz of traffic, watched the stars twinkle faintly in the hazy night sky. The room was the same, the sounds were the same, the view out the window the same.

Thank God, she'd changed, though. She was ready for a new life.

THE NEXT MORNING, Kimberly swung open the door to Life Dates and hummed a Norah Jones tune as she traipsed inside.

"Good morning, Maurice! Am I late?"

He didn't look up from the computer where he was typing. "Of course."

"Good, because I'd hate to shock you *too* much this morning."

He looked up, did a dramatic double take. "That dress, the *hair*!"

She'd dug through the clothes in the back of her closet this morning and picked out a bright, flowery dress and a pair of red shoes that matched the roses in the print.

"The dress and shoes were my Easter brunch outfit last year, and the hair, well, you're the one who was desperate to sever the bun."

"This boy's desperate no more!" He clutched his hand to his chest. "Your hair is positively *darling* with that flowing, shoulder-length look. Gwyneth Paltrow, step aside."

"What happened to Cameron Diaz? Charlize Theron?"

"Passé, dear! Gwyneth is in."

She laughed, helped herself to a handful of soy thingies.

"And you're laughing!"

She shot him a look. "Maurice, I think you need to get out more."

"I am out. Darling, it's not that you don't have a sense of humor, it's just that you've always held back from laughing out loud! I like this new, unrepressed fashion diva." He flashed her a knowing look. "That afternoon off did you a world of good, hmm? And I'm dying to hear every raunchy little detail, but we'll save that for our champagne toast at your wedding reception because today is busy, busy. For starters, Angie Canavesio from the Barnet and Owens advertising agency called. Her assistant is dropping off something. And I need to wrap up this month's account receivables by the end of the business day."

She passed a hand over her eyes. Angie. The Crusher commercial. Kimberly had been so caught up with Nigel, their evolving relationship, that she'd never discussed the results of the brainstorming session she'd had with the ad agency. Ideas Kimberly no longer wanted to pursue.

"Did Angie say what's being dropped off?"

"She was rushed, all chop-chop, had to get off the phone."

"Probably some contracts." Before Barnet and Owens's lawyers started working on rights to that Crusher footage, Kimberly would call Angie, suggest they brainstorm other ideas. While she was at it, she'd call Nigel, too. It had only been hours, but it felt like days since she'd seen him.

She headed to her office door, then paused. "Do me a favor?"

"Anything."

"Bring me a tofu burrito? I'm starved."

Maurice stopped typing and looked at her. "Darling, I thought I'd never hear you say the words. Let me finish this receivable, then I'll gleefully do your bidding."

TWENTY MINUTES LATER, Nigel walked into Life Dates.

Maurice, the phone receiver to his ear, smiled and mouthed "Go on in" while motioning to Kimberly's closed door.

Nigel nodded, paused at the crystal bowl and helped himself to one of the soy treats. When she'd called him earlier, he admitted he'd been sitting next to the phone, getting ready to call her, too, for no other reason than he missed her, wanted to see her. Like immediately, if not sooner.

She'd laughed, told him to drop by the office for a cup of coffee. Or tea, if Maurice has his way.

Nigel headed to her office door, remembering the first time he was here. He'd been dragging his feet for weeks about signing up with a dating agency and it hadn't helped that after he'd gotten the balls to do it, a certain Ms. Kimberly Logan was nearly an hour late. He'd sat in there and stewed, toyed with leaving, but stayed put. And good thing he had. He'd have missed out on meeting her.

And falling in love with her.

Wanted to love her the rest of her days, too, if she'd have him.

He opened the door and stopped in his tracks. Emotion crowded his heart as, for an unguarded moment, they bathed in each other's gazes. Kimberly looked as bright and fresh as the bouquet of irises on her desk. She wore a pretty flowered dress, her blond hair smooth and golden to her shoulders.

"You look beautiful."

She smiled, a bit shyly, but obviously pleased at his reaction.

"In fact," he continued, stepping inside and shutting the door behind him, "you look like the description I wrote for 'The Woman of my Dreams' in my enrollment form for Life Dates."

"*Look* like?"

He crossed behind her desk, stopped in front of her. "You *are* the woman of my dreams."

She angled her head up and he gazed into her eyes, liking the softness that shone in those winter-gray depths. Liked the sun-kissed pink of her skin, the way her blond hair framed her face. She was like a flower that had been holding its closed-tight petals, and now she was finally open, revealing all her hidden beauty.

"It's so good to see you," she whispered, touching his face.

Just a touch, and yet it tore through him with the power of lightning.

He caught her hand, so small it felt smothered by his. He drew her hand to his lips and kissed each fingertip.

"Ah, Kimberly." He hauled her into his arms, liking how sweetly resilient her body felt against his. He rested his head on hers, thinking nothing in the world felt better than to be with her.

He pulled back, holding her at an arm's distance and gave her a once-over. "Remember that night at Scarlett's, the bar where you coached me?"

"I think *you* did more coaching than I did."

He chuckled, thinking back to their hot first kiss. "That night, before I went inside, I remember wondering if you ever dressed up like this."

"This?"

"Softer, more feminine." He groaned. "Was that an insert-foot comment?"

"No." She hesitated. "There was a time I always dressed like this...." Her voice trailed off.

He wanted to know about that time, even as a part of him didn't. It hadn't been good, that much he knew. He sensed whatever had happened in her life had been as powerful as the forces that froze the Valley of Fire's sand dunes into petrified swirls of stone.

"A time before you rode the black horse out of town."

She nodded. "I was eighteen, married to a man who hadn't given up his single ways, to put it mildly. When I told him I knew there were other women, he said we could have stayed together if I'd kept pretending."

"Ouch."

"I knew by then marrying him had been a means to escape my house. Which, in retrospect, really hadn't been a bad place. Just one that hadn't recovered from the loss of its mother and wife." She paused. "Anyway, I got divorced. Looking back, I wish I'd returned home, mended things with my father. Instead I numbed myself to the pain of my failed marriage by becoming a party girl. It's one thing to be wild in a place like Vegas, quite another in a small town where everybody knows your business. By the time I left, I had quite the reputation. I've never for-given myself for the embarrassment I brought to my dad."

Nigel looked into her face, realizing how critical it'd been for her to reinvent herself, a skill she brought into Life Dates as she made over others.

"You've never gone back?" he asked gently.

"For my brother's wedding a few years ago, but…"

"You and your father didn't talk."

Her silence gave him the answer.

"Kimberly, sweetheart," he murmured, stroking her hair, "it's never too late to make amends. You've changed a lot lately. Grown softer. I bet your heart's softened, too. Maybe it's ready to bridge the gap with your father."

She leaned back, met his gaze. "And I thought I was the one who studied psychology."

"Maybe you're rubbing off on me."

For a moment, they stared openly into each oth-er's eyes with no need to hide what they felt.

"Speaking of how a person dresses and behaves," she said, easing on to another subject, "I should never have messed with perfection. You're a fantastic bad boy, but I miss the guy who wears those rooster-something-leg T-shirts."

A grin sauntered across his lips. "Foghorn Leghorn."

"Right. And the man who bakes brownies and sits by the phone. That man is every woman's dream. Dressing you up was fun, and don't get me wrong, you look meltdown hot in those body-molding clothes we bought, but Nigel—" she bit back emotion "—you're a catch just as you are."

He traced her trembling lips with the crook of his finger. "Then catch me," he whispered.

There was so much he wanted to say, but this wasn't the moment. He wanted a different ambience, a place where they were completely alone, before he opened his heart and expressed everything he yearned to share with this woman.

Knock knock knock.

"Come in, Maurice," Kimberly called out.

Maurice opened the door and held up his hands, one holding a foil-wrapped cylinder, the other a videotape. "Tofu burrito, and a videotape that Angie's assistant just dropped off. Attached note asks if you'll review ASAP, then call Angie."

"No contracts?"

"Right." Maurice shrugged. "Video probably contains samples of the agency's work. Maybe she wants to see if you'd like any of the concepts for your ad."

"Perfect. I left a message for Angie that I wanted to brainstorm some new ideas, so this is excellent timing."

Maurice walked across the room and set the burrito on her desk. "Shall I put this in the video player?"

She looked up at Nigel. "Do you mind?"

"Have you ever thought that maybe I'm interested in all aspects of your life?" He smiled at her in such a shy, hopeful way, she found herself grinning back like a love-struck teenager.

Something not missed by Maurice who slid her a

"you go girl" look as he crossed to a corner bookshelf and slipped the video into the VCR unit of the TV.

The TV screen blipped. Black-and-white lines rolled on its screen.

"Remote should be on your desk," Maurice said as he exited, closing the door behind him.

Nigel slipped into the guest chair, patting his lap for Kimberly to sit. She did, cuddling into Nigel's embrace as the image on the screen sharpened.

Angie's head came into focus, flashing those big white teeth. "Hi, Kimberly!"

Kimberly blinked at Nigel. "A personal message on a videotape?"

"Doesn't she believe in phone calls?"

Kimberly laughed, liking their comfortable camaraderie.

"Although talking's good," Angie said, "visuals are even better and I thought you'd appreciate seeing some ideas for your television commercial."

Kimberly felt a trickle of foreboding, glanced at her desk for the remote. She started to reach for it.

"Yesterday we discussed your audience—Vegas singles, especially the late-night casino workers. These people know the heart and guts of Vegas, so we don't need to hit them over the head with flash. And although we talked about hitting them with 'brazen,' that's really too narrow a focus."

Kimberly dropped her hand as she eased out a stream of pent-up breath. Just as Maurice had surmised, Angie was simply testing some new ideas. She snuggled closer against Nigel.

"What I was thinking," Angie continued, not a hair of her stylish do out of place, "was more of a chic-to-primitive approach. Something that would appeal to the spectrum of prospective clients' tastes."

Angie motioned to someone off camera. "So let's imagine the commercial kicking off with a tight shot on your head while you're extolling the virtues of Life Dates. Don't worry, we'll script something snazzy for you."

"What, they don't trust you?" asked Nigel.

"Maybe they're afraid I'll turn into a motormouth."

"And such a pretty motormouth, too."

Kimberly slid him an appreciative look as Angie's voice chippered on.

"...and after your intro, the camera will pull back and viewers will see a nicely dressed gentleman standing next to you. This will be the chic part."

Sure enough, a handsome man dressed in a suit stood next to Angie.

Angie gave him a once-over. "He'll be wearing a tux, though. Classical music in the background. Then, you'll waltz off the screen with him as the background changes from city to a desert scene."

"You know how to waltz?" asked Nigel.

Kimberly winced.

They watched as Angie and the man waltzed off-screen as the backdrop evolved into a desert scene. Molded sand dunes, blue skies.

Off camera, Angie's voice. "And one of the sand dunes will become…"

The image shrank until it became obvious it was a man's sculpted pec.

"This is the primitive part," murmured Angie. "Sexy, primal. The brazen part of 'what happens here, stays here.'"

The camera kept slowly pulling back, divulging inch by inch a man's oiled, muscled body wearing nothing but a black Speedo and a black mask.

Nigel as The Phantom.

Nigel stiffened. "What the—?" He straightened, glaring at the screen. "It's me in that Crusher commercial."

He turned to her, his eyes blazing. "Why are they using that old commercial?"

"Maybe they accidentally…" Kimberly swallowed, hard. Accidentally, her ass. She was trying to sugarcoat this, pretend she wasn't partially responsible. She grappled with how to explain as the footage kept rolling….

And rolling….

A greased-down, muscle-rippling Phantom carrying the swooning damsel across the burning sands, crushing her into his embrace. The classical music had segued into pounding jungle drums.

A creeping coldness crept over Kimberly's body. She felt unable to move, think.

"As you and I discussed, Kimberly," Angie continued off camera, "our lawyers are still pursuing rights to use this film. Fortunately, we were allowed to use this footage for this demo only. As you and I agreed, it's important for viewers to get an eyeful of The Phantom's hunky bod. The creative department is thinking maybe we'll morph your face onto the woman in his arms. Then, as he carries you off to the simmering sunset, you'll do a wrap-up about Life Dates catering to the chic and the primitive."

Kimberly came out of her frozen state and jumped up from Nigel's lap.

Angie laughed. "I tell you, if I had a stud muffin like that as my customer, it'd be hard to keep my mind on work. But as you said, Kimberly, he's just your client. No more, no less than dozens of others."

The screen went black as Kimberly punched the Off button on the remote.

Silence filled the room. With great effort, she looked from the screen to Nigel's face. "It's not what you think."

He stared at her for a long, steely moment. The blue eyes that had looked at her shyly only moments before were now cold as ice.

"I don't have to *think* anything." He motioned to the TV. "It was all right there." He paused, his voice dropping to a gruff whisper. "Did you really tell her there was nothing between us?"

Kimberly looked stricken. "I can explain…"

Nigel held up his hand in a stopping motion as his heart slowed to a sickening pace. He'd been so sure that she was different. That underneath those all-business suits and that uptight persona beat the heart of a woman who simply wanted to love and be loved. He thought back to yesterday, and how magical, inevitable and *right* it'd felt when he'd told her he loved her.

And she'd said she loved him, too.

But now, in the stark light of this room, he realized she wasn't any different than the women who'd tipped their way backstage after a match to meet The Phantom. He was a commodity. Someone to use.

He stood, crossed his arms. "First, explain why you're using me in that commercial."

She licked her lips. "We discussed using a portion of the Crusher commercial at our meeting, but I said I wanted to talk to you first—"

"Explain 'discussed.'"

"Angie recognized you in the waiting area, mentioned how effective it would be to involve you."

"Even knowing how that commercial was humiliating for me, something I regretted ever doing, you agreed."

Kimberly stared at him, the answer in her eyes.

He clenched his jaw, hating the next question, but he had to ask. "*Now* explain why you denied our relationship."

"I got caught up in the moment, wanted the agency to be successful…." Her voice broke.

Nigel swallowed back the bitter taste of being deceived. "You betrayed me a few hours before we made love. Before we admitted we loved each other."

"Nigel, *you* said you didn't want to talk business—"

"Or was it making love?" he interrupted, hurt pooling cold and black in his gut. He regretted what they'd shared, wished he'd never met her.

He looked around the room at the expensive lamps, sleek glass-and-chrome desk, top-of-the-line ergonomic chair. "You're a successful businesswoman, Kimberly, I just hadn't realized how far you'd go to be successful. So tell me, how many clients did you do this with? How many is 'no less than dozens of others?'"

"That's outrageous—"

"Tell you what. I won't stand in your way of using that commercial. After all, you *earned* it."

Her eyes brimming with tears, she took a step forward. "Please, don't. I was going to tell the ad agency to can the idea anyway. I had no idea what was on that video—"

"You could have canned the idea the moment it was hatched. Don't play heroine now. Face it, Kimberly, what matters to you is money, not people. And most surprising, you're willing to forfeit your reputation to get it. Seems to me you're still riding that black horse."

He watched the color leave her beautiful face. The face he'd kissed, caressed, held in his hands when he'd…

"Nigel," she choked, "you're wrong."

He snorted something unintelligible, pain tearing at his heart. More than anything, he wished he was wrong.

"You were right when you said the problem with me and love is that I've been too available. Well, Kimberly, I was too available to you, but not anymore."

He started to walk out, stopped at the door. Without looking at her, he said over his shoulder, "What I'd wanted to talk about was that last step. I was ready to pick the One."

With a disgusted shake of his head, he walked out the door.

KIMBERLY FELT STUNNED. How could something so right—so perfect—go wrong so quickly?

Her feet were cemented to the floor. All she could do was stare at the door, amazed he'd walked out. Hoping he'd come back, say he'd judged her too quickly.

He didn't even hear me out. He guts me, then walks.

She knew Nigel could be tough, but never realized how titanic the man's full presence could be until now. When he felt wronged, he was a power to be reckoned with.

She wrapped her arms around herself, as though that could soothe the hurt of her heart ripping in two.

For one frantic moment, she thought about running after him.

She closed her eyes and breathed in deeply. No, that'd be dumb. He was furious, she was damn near stupefied with regret. They'd clash, or weather agonizing moments of chilly silence.

If only she could turn back the clock and change the past. Instead of being caught up in Angie's razzmatazz about Vegas and brazen advertising, Kimberly could have nixed the idea of using Nigel.

He was right. Kimberly had let the notion of making money override her heart.

But he also could have let her explain.

Although if he walked back in here right now, she'd probably go ballistic for that alone. He *hadn't* let her get a word in edgewise. He'd wielded his sense of injustice over her without giving her a moment of mercy.

But all the internalizing over who said what, when and why, didn't change the fact she'd just lost the best thing that had come into her life in a long, long time.

"Kimberly?" Maurice stepped into the doorway, looking stricken. "What happened?"

She forced herself to sound lighthearted. "I think you'd better cancel the wedding caterers." Oh, to hell with that. "He—" she cleared her throat "—he walked out on me."

Maurice frowned, looked at the blackened TV screen, the remote still in her hand. "The video?"

She nodded. "I screwed up. Big-time."

"Oh, honey." His eyes did that puppy-dog thing that made her insides collapse. "Can you call him and explain?"

She turned to her desk, tossed the remote onto a pile of papers. "I hate this business."

"Darling, you're overreacting."

"I mean it, Maurice," she said, walking slowly around the office, looking at the symbols of her so-called success. "I've been too caught up in my work. Made it my life because I don't have a life. Then a man walks in who's willing to love me with his big, wonderful heart for the rest of my days and what do I do?"

Maurice wiped at his eye. "Honey, stop—"

"I betrayed him!"

"You didn't mean to," Maurice said in a strained voice. Wagging his hands in a "don't talk" gesture, he quickly crossed to the box of tissues on her desk, pulled one out. "Need one?"

She stopped walking and nodded.

He started to pull another out, sighed dramatically. "Oh, screw it." He picked up the entire box and headed to her.

"Okay," he said, holding out the box, "let's take the stance that you didn't mean to betray him, but you did. How do we patch this up?"

"We?"

"Don't forget I'm your best man of honor, a position I refuse to surrender."

She helped herself to a tissue. "I—we—can never patch this up. He wants nothing to do with me."

"He's a sensitive man." Maurice lowered her a look. "Trust me, I can tell these things. How about we send him a big box of chocolates?"

"Too much sugar." The memory of all the times Nigel chided her for her lousy diet brought a fresh swell of tears. She dabbed at her eyes, fighting the urge to wail like a banshee.

"Would jelly beans help? I could run out, buy a few dozen."

She snorted a laugh that was more a sob. "I hate this business. No, I hate myself. Success coach, hell. I was willing to make myself look like a whorehouse madam with that damn Crusher commercial. Get me my black horse, Maurice, I'm ready to ride again."

"Madam? Black horse?" His eyebrows knitted together in confusion. "Let's stick to the current topic. We're discussing ways to make up, get back your man."

"I've hated this business for a long time but just didn't know until this moment. I want to be a shrink instead."

"Jelly beans with a martini back. Whattaya say?"

She grabbed another tissue, blew her nose. "I don't want to manipulate people anymore. I want to inspire them, help them fulfill their potential, not tell them what they should wear, how to act, just so they can woo the opposite sex."

"But, Kimberly, think of all the people you matchmaked who fell in love and are happily married."

She paused. "I could've had that, too, but I blew it." When Maurice started to protest again, she raised her hand. "This is it, Maurice. I'm through."

"Through?"

"I'm selling Life Dates."

12

Six months later

NIGEL WALKED THROUGH the blistering August heat
into the Bellagio Gallery of Fine Art Museum. Today
was a scorcher. The kind of heat that sucked the color
out of the landscape and drained people of energy.

Although he was dressed to the bare minimum in
a Foghorn Leghorn T-shirt, a pair of cargo shorts and
flip-flops, he sighed with satisfaction at the onslaught
of air-conditioning as he entered the museum lobby.
This was the first time he'd been back to the Bellagio
since that night with Kimberly when she'd brought
him here as his success coach, and after getting jealous over those bar babes, played a sexily clad Anna
to his King of Siam.

He'd rented *Anna and the King of Siam* a few
months after that, curious who those characters were.
Afterward, he wished he and Kimberly had had the
same happy ending.

Pulling off his sunglasses, Nigel looked around.
Across the room, a boy waved.

Nigel smiled. Austin. Wearing a *buttoned* Hawaiian shirt. Was he getting taller by the week or was it Nigel's imagination?

He headed to where Austin stood next to the ticket counter.

"You're early," Nigel said, pulling out his wallet.

"I already got the tickets."

Nigel paused.

"I didn't pawn anything."

"I wasn't thinking that." *Just wondering where you got the money.* An old habit, worrying about Austin, hoping he was staying the course.

"Today students get in free, and my allowance covered your ticket. So my treat."

Nigel slipped the wallet back into his pocket. *Got to stop being hypervigilant with the boy.* Austin was gaining confidence, doing better in school, even had a steady girlfriend who made straight As. "Thanks. I'll get lunch afterward."

"Cool."

Austin handed Nigel his ticket as they walked toward the exhibit. "Thought you'd never get here."

"Am I late?" Nigel glanced at the large clock on the wall. Noon on the dot. "We said twelve, right?"

"Yeah. Just kidding."

"Keeping me on my toes, eh?"

Austin slid him a teasing look. "Somebody's gotta."

Nigel wasn't sure when their relationship slid from confrontational into camaraderie, but he wasn't going to second-guess it. On a few occasions, Austin had even called him at home, once just to say "hi" which left Nigel feeling even taller than his six-five.

For the next hour, they walked through the exhibit and discussed paintings. Nigel was impressed with Austin's insights and comments about the artists' use of color and technique. They'd been visiting different museums off and on for the past six months, ever since Kimberly suggested it that day when they visited the Valley of Fire. She'd been right. Austin loved it. Nigel had followed up on another of her suggestions and enrolled him in art classes. So far, he'd studied pastels and was now discovering watercolor.

Somewhere in the process, Austin stopped talking about getting another tattoo.

After the exhibit, they sat down to lunch at Café Bellagio, taking in the sweet scents of flowers from the nearby botanical gardens.

"Can't wait for the weather to lighten up so we can have our picnics again," commented Austin while checking out the menu. He quickly looked up. "Not that being here isn't cool. I just liked being outdoors, too, you know?"

"Me, too," Nigel said.

They read the menu in silence against a background of muted chatter and clinking glasses. A jazz instrumental played over the audio system.

Austin flipped back his neatly tied ponytail. "You ever see her?"

Nigel met Austin's gaze. Those dark eyes, older than their years, took Nigel aback for a moment.

"No," he finally answered.

"Why not?"

After that picnic in February, Kimberly had never joined them again. Austin had asked about her a few times, but stopped after Nigel kept mumbling the same "It's over" response. Nigel hadn't wanted to talk about it. Still didn't.

Although in his gut he knew it was wrong to dismiss her that easily. Austin had already had too many people dismissed in his young life—his biological father, the men who flowed in and out of his mother's life, even Austin himself had been dismissed by the system before that judge gave him a break. For the boy to ask about Kimberly after all this time meant he didn't want to write her off with a curt "It's over."

"Because…" Nigel looked back at his menu, the words blurring into each other. "Because we reached a point where…"

It still hurt like hell. Maybe he understood why the boy was asking, but it didn't mean he was ready to reopen an old wound. He pushed aside his utensils and laid his menu on the table. "Why the sudden interest?"

Austin shrugged. "I wanted to tell her something."

After six months? "You could call her at her business."

"Life Dates, right?"

"Right."

"It's closed."

Nigel's insides contracted.

At that moment, a waiter approached their table.

A twentysomething in a designer dress shirt accented with a black silk tie that matched his chinos. "May I take your order?"

Nigel mindlessly scanned the menu again. *What happened to Kimberly's business?* "Uh, I need a few minutes."

"No problem, take your time. I'll be back." The waiter headed to another table where a gentleman was flagging him down.

Nigel looked at Austin. "Life Dates is closed?"

"I guess. When you dial the number, you get a 'this number's been disconnected' recording."

Kimberly loved her business. Lived and breathed it. Nigel couldn't imagine what she'd do with herself if she wasn't pouring her energy into it.

"You have her home number?" asked Austin. "I called Information but she's not listed."

"Not anymore." He puffed out a breath. "I, uh, threw away the card with her number on it."

"Man, you should've held on to it."

Nigel had often thought the same thing. Typically late at night when he was alone with his thoughts and his loneliness, and the world mocked him with what he'd lost. He'd see her sparkling eyes in a starry sky, swear he heard her whisper on a passing breeze. And he'd look at the moon and remember her face, hurt and pale, when he walked out on her.

I did the right thing. I deserve better than a woman who didn't want me for myself.

If he was so right, why did it still haunt him?

"You think I screwed up?"

Austin drew his lips in thoughtfully. "She was a nice lady."

"So," Nigel said, shifting in his seat, "you want to tell her something?"

"Yeah. I tried out for soccer. Practice begins in a few weeks, right before school starts."

Nigel blinked, grinned. "Congratulations, son!"

A look of surprise crossed the boy's face, and Nigel knew what they both were thinking. Father. Son. A subject he wanted to pursue someday soon.

The waiter reappeared, took their order.

After he left, Nigel took a deep breath. "I'll do what I can."

Austin picked up his water glass. "What?"

"I'll do what I can to get her number for you."

Austin took a sip, set the glass back down. "Hey, while you're at it, get it for yourself, too."

KIMBERLY STOOD BEHIND the wooden podium and looked out at the people who sat in rows of folding chairs in the hotel conference room.

"The last step," she said, "is to pick the One. And that means *you*. Make a to-do list of things to enjoy, things to love and put yourself first. Never forget— you're number one."

The audience broke into applause. After thanking them, and reminding them of her Web site address where tapes of this talk could be purchased, Kimberly stepped down and joined the crowd.

"Nice job, Gwyneth," said Maurice, sidling up to her.

She hugged him. "Thanks for showing up, giving your support." She shook someone's hand, thanked another, then slipped her arm through Maurice's and headed to a table set up with tea, coffee, cans of soda.

After closing down Life Dates five months ago, Kimberly did something she'd been thinking about for a long time. She designed a program to motivate and inspire people to change themselves, at their own pace, when they were ready. She called her new business "Life Gates" after a series of "gates" on which she founded one's personal growth with different six-step programs for different life circumstances. Today she'd given a talk on "How to Make a Good Life."

She still viewed herself as a success coach, but with changing a person from the inside out, not the outside in. She focused on people's passions, goals, dreams and how to make those a reality. Many of her former clients had signed up for seminars and workshops. As word spread, she'd been attracting new clientele.

They reached the table. Maurice poured hot water into his cup. "Kimberly?"

"Coffee."

He shot her a look.

"Maurice, this motivational speaker still needs her java fix. I'll keep it to a minimum, promise." She poured herself a cup. "So how's your business going?"

Maurice selected a tea bag, unwrapped it. "Just signed a lease for a one-man office near my condo. And I've decided on a name for my dating agency."

"And?"

"Boy Meets Boy. I already have ten clients."

"Good name." Kimberly had encouraged Maurice to start his own dating agency that catered to the gay community. He knew the business, the lifestyle— it was a win-win combination.

"At this rate, you'll soon be hiring an office manager. I suggest someone who stocks healthy snacks, has a droll sense of humor, is a good dresser, plus a perfectionist streak wouldn't hurt."

"Make that *fabulous* dresser, darling." He paused, smiled. "You're a dynamite coach, Kimberly. I've always wanted to run my own business and thanks to your guidance, it's now a reality."

"Wonderful."

As he dipped the tea bag into his cup, the scent of chamomile traced the air. "Speaking of wonderful, have you—?"

This came up every single time she and Maurice talked.

"No."

"Why not?"

"Because."

"Because he's *perfect* for you, darling, and trust me, that man is too proud to contact you. Time for you to take the first step before it's too late."

"It probably is. After all, it's been six months."

As usual, Maurice just ignored whatever reason or excuse she gave and launched into *his* reasons why she needed to be assertive and go "after her man."

"After listening to your talk today, I was thinking how those six 'How to Make a Great Life' steps can be applied to your getting back together with Nigel. Let's see, step one, dress for a great life. Well, you look positively smashing in these *Roman Holiday* sundresses you're wearing this summer. And remember, first impressions are everything."

"Maurice, the man is furious at what I did, we've discussed this before—"

"Step two," he continued, "act for a great life. You certainly are doing that with your new business and approach to life." He frowned. "What were the rest of the old steps?"

With a roll of her eyes, she repeated, "Three, make women melt. Four, kiss her 'til she whimpers. Five, love her 'til she screams. Six, pick 'The One.'"

"Whoa, dearest, you should keep those in your *new* steps because they'd definitely make a great life."

She laughed. "I don't think so—"

He waved a hand in the air. "Yes, yes, now listen up. I have a little gift for you." He handed her a brown paper bag. "Inside is a foolproof recipe for something that will win back his heart."

She shook her head. "Maurice—"

He gave her that puppy-dog look she'd never been able to resist.

"Kimberly, darling, let me be *your* success coach.

Just try this, that's all I'm asking. Aren't you always telling people these days to go after their dreams?"

"Yes, but—"

"Then go after yours. Go after that delicious man who got away. You know I'll never give up."

"That's the part that scares me."

"Good." He patted the bag. "I want a full report in the morning. At the very least, I expect you to tell me you were kissed 'til you whimpered."

"You're impossible."

NIGEL STOOD IN THE KITCHEN and admired his new table, the last piece to complete the renovation of the room. Its rich rosewood sheen complemented the white tile flooring accented with triangles of burnt almond. Rigo insisted the color was brown, but Nigel wouldn't budge on burnt almond.

He wasn't sure what room he wanted to tackle next. Today during lunch at the museum, he'd asked Austin if he'd like to come over and paint one of the rooms. It might not be a wholly artistic endeavor, but Nigel figured the boy might enjoy picking out the color and making a room come to life with it.

The front doorbell rang.

He checked the clock on the stove. 5:00 p.m. A little late for the postman. Probably Rigo dropping by.

Nigel padded across the living-room carpet to the front door. During the summers, he liked to kick off his shoes when he got home and walk around barefoot.

He opened the door. His heart dropped.

"Hi," said a soft, familiar voice.

It was like seeing a vision from six long months ago. She wore a billowy summer dress with little spaghetti straps that showed off her creamy shoulders. A pair of heeled sandals exposed her pink-tipped toenails.

And the hair, ah, the hair. It was slightly longer and fell loose in sleek golden waves.

After a beat, she said, "I brought you something."

He'd been so caught up looking her over, he'd missed that she was holding an aluminum-foil covered pan. Hell, he hadn't even said hello.

"Hello."

She smiled tentatively, although her eyes looked a little strange and he wondered if she was going to cry. But she didn't.

She extended the pan.

He accepted it. "Thanks."

He stood there, his fingers fidgeting underneath the glass, not sure what to say, wishing he could have a beer or a cold shower or something to quell his rattled nerves. At least it was relatively comfortable on his front porch as the awning offered some respite from the late-afternoon sun.

Her facial expression shifted. Instead of looking as though she might cry, she suddenly looked purposeful. As if she was going to say something.

He waited.

Her lips parted.

He leaned slightly forward.

Nothing.

Kimberly's insides were knotted so tight, it was a miracle blood was still flowing. She'd walk away but her feet had become one with the cement and all she could do was stare at a surprised Nigel holding a pan which contained the first thing she'd baked in years.

The instant she got home—God willing she could eventually pull her act together, walk to the car and drive—she was going to call Maurice and tell him offering brownies to a shell-shocked Nigel was the worst idea since Eve offered the apple.

Swallowing her heart back down her throat, she looked into his eyes. Those impossibly blue eyes. Her gaze dropped over the dramatic line of his jaw, down to that cocky cartoon rooster on his T-shirt. *And to think I insisted those shirts had to go if he wanted to woo a woman. Oh, me of little faith.*

Her gaze drifted lower, past the shorts and over his tanned, molded thighs down to his bare feet.

A crazy thought zapped through her mind.

That afternoon in the Jeep, she'd seen all of him naked except for his feet, which had been braced somewhere against the floorboard.

That afternoon. If there was a singular point in her life she would always remember, it'd be their fierce and passionate lovemaking that day in the Valley of Fire. His body moving into hers, that deep voice whispering sweet, sensual secrets. Their confession of love.

"What is it?" Nigel asked.

Heat flooded her face. "N-nothing."

He frowned, lifted the pan.

"Oh. Brownies."

"Brownies?"

He started to say something but seemed to think better of it, but she knew what he was thinking. How, way back when, she'd coached him to stop baking for his crushes. Maurice was smart picking up this mix. Her making a batch was a positive statement to Nigel that his efforts had been right-on, and her efforts to change him had been, well, foolish.

He was perfect just as he was.

"They're, uh, not from scratch," she said, gesturing toward the pan. "Box mix." Amazing she could stand in front of a room of two hundred and blithely work her way through a talk, but here in front of Nigel she could barely form coherent strings of words.

"Can't go wrong with box mixes."

Another stare-down.

"Would you…like to come inside?"

They shared a look and she knew they were thinking the same thing. That night when they were first intimate, she'd shown up on his doorstep, surprising him then, too. And after she'd gone inside, it hadn't been that long before their passion exploded. How many times had she thought back to that night, remembering every detail, wishing she could turn back time and start over with this man.

He stepped back, ushering her inside.

Her breath caught in her throat as, for a crazy moment, she wondered if she'd have that chance again.

She paused inside the front door, luxuriating in the frosted waves of air-conditioning rippling over her heated skin. She looked around, remembering the first time she'd seen his place she'd sworn it looked supersize. She glanced past the couch at all the photos, wondering if any new ones had been added. Like pictures of a current girlfriend?

Kimberly drew a breath and released it, telling herself she wouldn't be disappointed if there were. After all, he was a good-looking, sincere man with a supersize heart. If a woman had her head on straight, *this* was the kind of guy to go after, not some self-absorbed, baby-I'm-too-good-for-you bad boy.

"I still live in a sea of photos," he said, following her gaze.

"I didn't get to really look at them before."

The word "before" hung in the air as they shared another knowing look.

"Would you like to now?"

Every single one. "Oh, yes, I love family photos."

"Odd that you only have one. I mean, your loving them and all."

The photo of her family that he'd looked at that night at her place. Recently she'd realized that the past wasn't as daunting as it'd once been, and reminders didn't carry the same weight. Sometimes she wondered if letting go of who she thought she should be had helped her let go of other baggage she didn't need to carry anymore. Wouldn't Nigel be surprised to know she was planning a trip home soon, too.

He lead the way around the living room, holding the brownie pan with one hand while the other pointed out his sisters, father, mother, a gaggle of aunts and cousins.

At the end, he gestured to a silver-framed photo of a woman who looked to be in her seventies. He introduced her as his grandmother, Alice.

"She looks so sweet," said Kimberly, checking out the endearing smile in the wizened face framed with white-blue hair.

"Oh, she could be, except if she was laying down the law. She once told me that if I ever took advantage of a woman under the influence, she'd personally hunt me down like a dog and string me up."

"Your *grandmother* said that?"

"She had her moments."

They were standing so close, Kimberly could smell his clean, masculine scent. Could see the ripples of movement beneath his muscled arms. And within those eyes, she swore she caught a telltale glint of interest that turned her shivery inside.

He broke the silence. "Want a brownie?"

"No."

He looked taken aback before a grin slow-danced across his lips. "Come on, I bet they're good."

"I didn't know you were a betting man."

He looked at her in an old familiar way that made her wonder if he'd missed her as deeply as she him.

For an agonizing moment she toyed with dropping her guard and saying what was in her heart, what had been on her mind these past six months. That she'd been wrong, so wrong agreeing to the ad agency's idea. That she loved him. Loved that rock-bottom quality of his voice, the way he carried himself in the world, how he treated others. Loved his protective instincts and even, that last sad afternoon she'd seen him, his stubborn insistence that his integrity was not to be compromised.

And, oh, how she'd loved the ways he'd made her feel.

Maybe it wasn't too late. Maybe they had a second chance.

"I'd love a brownie."

"Okay," he said slowly, hesitating as though she might change her mind again. When she didn't, he continued, "That's good. Gives me an opportunity to show off my newly remodeled kitchen."

When they got there, she stopped and uttered an admiring sound.

"It's so you," she said on a release of breath. The room was strongly masculine with stylistic touches that reflected his sensitive nature.

"Think so?"

"Oh, yes." She walked around the patterned tile floor, checked out the bay window over the sink with several pots of herbs on its ledge, the mix of wood and marble countertops. "Everything is you..." She suddenly stopped and gestured toward the far wall.

"…except for that purple color. That's more me." She dropped her hand. "I mean—"

"No, it's true," he said gently. "It is you."

He set the pan down on the table, took a step toward her, then stopped. He folded his arms and leaned against a chair.

"The color's called Royal Plum. I thought of you when I picked it out, and a pal of mine kept reminding me it was you every time he stuck his nose into my business."

"What?"

"You know how friends can be when they have matchmaking on their minds."

She laughed. "Oh, don't I know." *Do you still want us?*

The air-conditioning hummed. Outside the window, a hummingbird hovered in a flash of color, then zipped away.

And in that moment, Kimberly thought about lost opportunities. For all the words in her mind, all the needs in her heart, she was choosing to stand here and chat about inconsequential things and possibly lose the best thing that had ever walked into her life.

"Nigel—"

"Kimberly—" he said at the same time. "You first."

"Have you changed?" Her heartbeat thundered in her ears. "I mean—"

"Yes."

"Yes?"

"I'm still me, still love my Foghorn Leghorn Ts, but inside, my heart has changed."

Nigel paused, wondering if he was saying the wrong thing. Her mouth was slack, her eyes filled with questions, and he told himself to take this part slow. Too often in the past he'd misread signals, blurted things only to realize he'd misunderstood the situation.

Maybe he'd take a step back, go to a safe topic. "What happened to Life Dates?"

She flinched slightly, then cleared her face of emotion. "I sold it," she said matter-of-factly, that old professionalism creeping back into her tone. "To Maurice, actually, although we agreed I'd keep the name as my business had been identified with it for so long. I've altered it to Life Gates, a series of personal growth programs I've established."

"So you're a personal-growth coach?"

She smiled. "Yes, although I do very little one-on-one coaching anymore. I prefer to be a motivational speaker, running workshops and seminars. I've even taken my six-step programs and reworked them into the different 'gates' of life."

"Sounds excellent."

"I enjoy inspiring people to change from the inside out, not vice versa." She swallowed back the emotion coursing through her. "You once accused me of caring more about money than people, and although that hurt, I've since decided you were partly right. Now I make less, but I enjoy life more. I like to think

I'm a little wiser, too." Her eyes glistened with emotion. "I'm sorry," she suddenly blurted. "I was wrong. That was so stupid of me, agreeing with that agency about their ideas for a commercial. At the very least, I should have talked to you—"

"I'm sorry, too," he said, moving closer and touching her arm. "It was stupid of me, too, to hold on to my pride."

Another silence ensued.

"So," he said, lowering his voice, "in your new six-step programs, do people still pick 'The One'?"

"Yes."

"I missed that step."

His eyes lowered to her soft, sweet mouth and, encircling her waist with his arm, he pulled her flush against him and gently kissed her forehead, each cheek, before brushing her mouth with his. She melted against him as his lips finally possessed hers—it'd been so long, too long.

With great effort, he broke the kiss and touched his forehead to hers.

"I love you," he said huskily. "I've never known a woman with such fire and beauty." He chucked softly. "Never known anyone as stubborn, either. I love your generous, courageous heart, Kimberly Logan. You broke through a boy's defenses and a man's loneliness, two guys who desperately want you back."

"Oh, Nigel, I love you, too." She paused, pulled her face back slightly and met his gaze. "Two guys?" A smile curved her lips. "Austin! How is he?"

"At least two inches taller, I swear. Taking art classes. Foregoing more tattoos. Wanting to call you with some news." When she started to speak, Nigel pressed a finger against her lips. "It's his news. You'll have to wait."

She wrapped her arms around Nigel's neck. "I waited six months to break the ice with you, I can wait for Austin's news."

"And I waited a long time to finish my program."

She blinked. "How to Make a Bad Boy? But that no longer applies to you."

He brushed a wisp of her hair off her cheek. "Oh, yes it does." Searching her eyes, he murmured, "Kimberly, you're the One. I pick you."

"Nigel, oh, Nigel, I pick you, too."

And they kissed until she whimpered.

AMERICAN HEROES

**These men are heroes—
strong, fearless...
And impossible to resist!**

Join bestselling authors Lori Foster, Donna Kauffman
and Jill Shalvis as they deliver up

MEN OF COURAGE

Harlequin anthology
May 2003

Followed by *American Heroes* miniseries
in Harlequin Temptation

RILEY by Lori Foster
June 2003

SEAN by Donna Kauffman
July 2003

LUKE by Jill Shalvis
August 2003

Don't miss this sexy new miniseries by some of
Temptation's hottest authors!

Available at your favorite retail outlet.

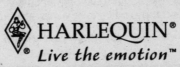

Visit us at www.eHarlequin.com

If you enjoyed what you just read,
then we've got an offer you can't resist!

Take 2 bestselling love stories FREE!

Plus get a FREE surprise gift!

Clip this page and mail it to Harlequin Reader Service®

IN U.S.A.	IN CANADA
3010 Walden Ave.	P.O. Box 609
P.O. Box 1867	Fort Erie, Ontario
Buffalo, N.Y. 14240-1867	L2A 5X3

YES! Please send me 2 free Blaze™ novels and my free surprise gift. After receiving them, if I don't wish to receive anymore, I can return the shipping statement marked cancel. If I don't cancel, I will receive 4 brand-new novels each month, before they're available in stores! In the U.S.A., bill me at the bargain price of $3.99 plus 25¢ shipping and handling per book and applicable sales tax, if any*. In Canada, bill me at the bargain price of $4.47 plus 25¢ shipping and handling per book and applicable taxes**. That's the complete price and a savings of at least 10% off the cover prices—what a great deal! I understand that accepting the 2 free books and gift places me under no obligation ever to buy any books. I can always return a shipment and cancel at any time. Even if I never buy another book from Harlequin, the 2 free books and gift are mine to keep forever.

150 HDN DZ9K
350 HDN DZ9L

Name	(PLEASE PRINT)	
Address	Apt.#	
City	State/Prov.	Zip/Postal Code

Not valid to current Harlequin Blaze™ subscribers.

Want to try two free books from another series?
Call 1-800-873-8635 or visit www.morefreebooks.com.

 * Terms and prices subject to change without notice. Sales tax applicable in N.Y.
** Canadian residents will be charged applicable provincial taxes and GST.
All orders subject to approval. Offer limited to one per household.
® and ™ are registered trademarks owned and used by the trademark owner and or its licensee.

BLZ04R   ©2004 Harlequin Enterprises Limited.

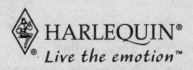

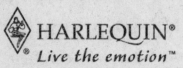